In The Dark

Sheila Peters

Contents

Prologue: Hana

T he bullet cracked into the air, accompanied by a sharp whistle. The noise heralded death and destruction, reverberating in the ears and setting off flocks of birds westwards towards the golden falling sphere.

Don't pay attention. It must have been the seventh gunshot today, or at least the seventh I heard. I whispered a small prayer, thanking God for not being at the receiving end of that monstrous contraption of death.

"Work faster," a low voice whispered into my ear, abruptly cutting my prayers short.

I stiffened, fearing the worst as I felt his body press against my back. Hurriedly, I tried to regain momentum sifting through the possessions of new prisoners, but he didn't seem to move. Instead, he rested a hand on my waist, sending shivers throughout my body. My breathing hitched but my hands didn't stop moving as I continued to put valuables in one basket and the excess in another.

Only through my peripheral vision could I tell that he was quite young. I didn't dare turn around to examine his features properly, mainly because I noticed he was in prestigious uniform and more so because I was certain that it was a gun pressed against my midriff and not any other innocuous object.

He lingered for a while, watching me work in close proximity despite there being at least thirty other women doing the same job. Barred between his tough chest and the stocked table, I felt immobile. I continued to work, trying my best to ignore his presence despite the reminder of his hand lightly sitting on my waist and his warm breath loitering around my neck.

What was he doing? He wasn't saying anything, nor did he seem concerned with the pace of my work anymore.

A few moments passed with only the sound of metal clinking or SS men stomping around filling the silence. Eventually, he relieved his hand off my waist and had walked away with nothing else to say. I exhaled in great relief, returning to work with full commitment, eager to not fall behind again.

As I continued to process the belongings, I couldn't help but catch glimpses of him. He walked in circles around the group of us prisoners in a measured yet imperious manner. Though he was notably younger than the several other SS officers standing around the area, he definitely attained a higher authority, visible in the way his uniform was decorated and in the way the other officers seemed more nervous today than every other day in which he wasn't here.

I found that my eyes had wondered to his face, which bore no smile, fitting well with the rest of his expressionless demeanour. His eyes were an arctic blue, glistening enough to be apparent from a distance, and were always focussed on the assembly of working women at hand. From time to time, I noticed his eyes fell on me, but only for split seconds. He had distinct cheekbones and an angular jaw that framed his youthful face and his pale skin seemed smoother than silk. His hair was not visible much under his peaked cap, but was a lustrous dark chocolate colour that seemed very soft to the touch.

I averted my eyes every time he would pass me, hoping he would give me no more attention the way he did before. I continued to work despite the prominent ache in my arms, managing to catch a few more glimpses of him as we walked round. The swastika was proudly displayed on his left sleeve and an Iron Cross on the chest pocket of his military coat alongside other ostentatious ornaments, as well as the gun perched on the left side of his belt.

A poster child for the tyrannous Nazi regime.

-

The following day obtained the same tiresome routine. In the morning, I had shovelling in the fields for the next rotation to come and plant vegetable seeds (to be used towards the war effort). Then in the evening there was processing belongings (in which yesterday I had my very strange encounter with the uniformed man) and after that I had to do the cleaning in the infirmary.

Another day at the camp once again left me exhausted and hungry. The meagre amount of soup they offered day combined with the laborious hours of work was bone shattering. When night fell and the clock chimed midnight to signal the end of a working day, I made my way to my allocated cabin with haste in anticipation to hold my mother and sister.

Mama and Lola were all I had left. Dad was gone, ripped away faster than I could have ever imagined. When we were admitted to the camp, we were stripped of all our possessions, left with nothing but a worn blouse and skirt and a single mattress to fit the three of us.

I wanted to leave. I wanted to go back home.

Nearing the doors to Cabin 14, I was halted in my tracks by a bony hand planting itself on my shoulder.

"Hana Amsel?" I turned around to view the Matron grabbing my attention. I nodded, unsure as to any reason why she would want to see me. "Come with me."

Chapter 1

After walking a mile or so, an extravagant mansion upreared itself amidst the thick forestry. Despite being heavily guarded by several SS officers, everything about it was beautiful; from the finely detailed window frames to the stunning fountain that centred in the driveway. Huge Swastika flags were paraded at the front, hanging out of each upper floor window like lions charging forward in battle.

For a moment, I was left in pure, undeniable awe. I grew up in a very working class borough of Berlin where houses like these only existed in dreams. However, Matron didn't let my moment of admiration last for long as she tugged my arm, forcing me to follow her through to back of the house.

We ended up in front of a door in the basement of the house, where I noticed masses of maids and other help scurrying around with baskets of dirty laundry or platters of exquisite dining and whatnot, busy at work despite it being very late at night. From a bundle of keys hanging off her waist, the Matron selected one and inserted it into the rusty keyhole of the door we were standing before.

"You have fifteen minutes." She opened the door, pushed me inside and said, "Make sure you look perfect," before slamming the door shut behind her.

I turned around and took a good look at the room, taken by full surprise at its contents. My jaw dropped, astounded to see so many commodities I had missed for so long.

There was a single shower that stood at the corner of the room and when I tried the tap, it rained fresh water and not the yellowing type served in the camps. Touching the clean water made me feel numb. It was a luxury now and to watch so much fall unused made my heart wrench. I quickly turned the tap off, eager to examine everything else in the room as well.

On top of the ceramic sink, there lay small bottles of shampoo, shower gel and body cream. I was stunned; the last time I used any of the three was almost a month ago, when I was a free person. Even a razor sat benignly amidst all the other treasures. I found my fingers lacing delicately through each of the items, still finding it difficult to process my new surroundings.

There was even a knee-length dress that hung from the coat hooks on a wooden hanger. A real dress, not a dreary uniform one. It was a gorgeous sapphire blue with three buttons at the front and didn't bare the red triangle to identify me as a German political prisoner, unlike my regular uniform. It was even accessorised with a pair of polished shoes and stockings.

I didn't question why I was here and why I was told to 'look perfect'. I just showered as fast as I could, as per my time constraints, and put on the dress, admiring how well it fit in the mirror. I noticed for the first time my collar bones visibly protruded out and the shape of my face narrowed under the lighting of the bathroom, but I brushed those thoughts aside.

I knocked on the door to signal that I was done and the Matron came to open it. She quickly checked to see the razor was not missing of a blade and when she was happy with what she saw and when she nodded to approve of how I looked, she tugged my arm roughly and rushed me up the grand stairs in the lavish house until we were in a bedroom on the first floor, one probably the size of my old house!

"Don't touch anything and don't steal anything either." Matron asserted. I had never stolen a thing in my life and I wasn't intending to start now despite how deprived I was. "Don't talk back, only speak if you're spoken to, do you get the idea?" I nodded, not any less confused. "And most of all, do exactly as you're told. Understand?"

I nodded once more with no extra knowledge as to whose orders I was going to be taking. It was nearing 1am by the clock on the wall and I could only wonder what was wanted of me.

"Good. Don't leave the room, he will be here soon."

"He? Who's he?" I questioned, eager to know who this mysterious person was. However, I was left in the dark as the Matron quickly exited the room with no other word.

Stranded in the room alone, I decided to look around, careful to not touch anything. The dark wooden floorboards contrasted the white walls in a very expensive manner. Around the room sat an oak cupboard and a neatly made double bed with two bedside tables, each with a lamp and one also with a vinyl player. There was a chaise lounge that sat in one corner as well as various other pieces of furniture. By my presumptions, it was a man's room, considering the number of cologne and cigars arranged on the dressing table. Though it was overall rather minimalistic, it seemed to scream luxury.

I walked over to an elegant bookshelf opposite the bed, half filled with books and little ornaments. The other half consisted of a multitude of vinyls lined up on several rows in an orderly fashion, full of colour. I walked over, admiring the arrangement of music, something that had sincerely shaped my childhood. But what caught my eye was a certain disk, the cover still distinguished in my memory, sitting comfortably at the end of one row. I picked it up, nostalgia swelling in my stomach.

'Sing, You Sinners' by the –

"High Hatters." If it weren't for my already iron grip on the sentimental vinyl, I most definitely would have dropped it out of shock.

I stood there, frozen, mouth ajar, hoping that I was not really seeing the dark haired, uniformed officer from yesterday leaning against the door-frame. His eyes travelled from his vinyl in my hands to my own eyes, inducing flames of fear in my stomach.

"I'm so sorry, I –"

"It's okay." I didn't know whether to be relieved or not. "You know the song?"

I looked down at the item in my hand, feelings of loss pulsing in my veins. "My father and I used to dance to it when I was a little girl," I answered, truthfully.

Memories of my father taking me to see my first movie came flooding back. It was called 'Honey', where I had first heard the song performed by Lillian Roth. I was seven at the time. And then, when I was eight, my father bought the High Hatters version on vinyl for my birthday, a gift he had saved up for for weeks. He used to play it on my grandfather's old vinyl player (which was slightly broken but we managed to make use of it) in our small living room and we would dance to it all night long until Mama would shout at us and tell us to go to sleep. But that was a life we lived before everything changed at home, and before foreign music became illegal under the policy of Gleichschaltung.

"B-but the Reichsmusikkammer will arrest you for having this and –" It was then that I realised what I said and who I was saying it to and instantly started regretting every decision I had ever made in my life.

I watched attentively, too frozen in a moment of utter horror to even be able to shake as he approached me, unhurriedly. His face was blank, emotionless, unreadable. But I knew he could sense the fear smeared all over my face. And the way he approached me stealthily, we both knew I was the prey and that he was most definitely the predator.

When he got near, he gently took the vinyl out of my hands but he didn't seem to stop coming closer. I clenched my fists as I felt his free hand fall to my waist whilst his face neared mine. He was in such close proximity that I could feel the heat radiating from his body. Though I couldn't see his face, I knew he wasn't pleased. The cold silence made me feel sick. I stiffened, not daring to move an inch.

"Then it's a damn good thing that they can't arrest me for something they don't know about." He whispered, a dark edge coating his tone. His words were imperative. His voice was so low that I would have missed it if his lips weren't so close to my ear.

And then, in a gradual motion, his face moved from the side of mine until we were facing each other, but not alleviating from the very close proximity. He was looking down at me from his height, making me feel even smaller. His sharp eyes bore into mine, danger and menace emanating from his orbs. I gulped, paralysed under his intimidating gaze.

"Understand?" I nodded, understanding exactly what he meant.

I was merely just a girl, no threat to him. I wouldn't have the guts to tell anyone because I knew anything that he could do to me would be ten times worse because I also knew he was already in too powerful of a position for something as trivial as this to get him imprisoned.

"Very good." He stated, curtly.

I watched as he took his jacket off and placed it across the chaise lounge. He looked much younger in less of the SS uniform. Without the peaked cap and the jacket, he was left in a black shirt. He looked around twenty, probably younger, but it was hard to tell through his concrete face.

I was lost as to what to do. He wasn't interacting with me and I was just standing there utterly confused. Out of curiosity, I looked at the bookshelf once more to witness the assemblage of vinyls sitting so innocently on the shelves, none of which actually seemed legal.

Swing music. Rows and rows full of swing music.

It came to me as a complete surprise when he took the 'Sing, You Sinners' vinyl out of the sleeve and placed it in the phonograph before putting the stylus down to let the music play.

I momentarily closed my eyes, taking in the sound I had unknowingly been yearning to hear since I was a little girl. The last time I heard this song was six years ago, just before the Nazis took full power. It reminded me of my father, now dead, who was once bursting with life and energy and happiness which fuelled our entire family, before he burnt out.

"Pour some whisky," he ordered, finally breaking the silence. He was lying down on his bed on top of the duvet, one ankle over the over, watching me intently.

Hesitant for a second, I looked around the room and spotted an expensive looking decanter resting on top of the table. I walked over to it and started pouring the brown translucent liquid into a glass. I picked it up and my hands were shaking. The liquid rocked in the whisky tumbler even when I was still and more so as I walked over to hand it to him.

The music was still playing, the only comfort I got in this abnormal situation. I was standing right next to his bed now, watching him swirl the drink in his glass with an unsatisfied look on his face.

"You didn't pour yourself one." His eyes flashed towards mine as I was taken aback by his statement. I didn't know what to say.

Was this why I was called here? Because he was lonely and just wanted a drinking partner?

"Go on, have a drink." He insisted.

I didn't want to. I wanted to go home. I wanted Mama.

"I don't –"

"Don't what? Follow orders?" He cocked an eyebrow.

My stomach knotted up as my mouth became dry. I didn't know what to do. But I did the only thing I could do and walked back to the decanter to pour another glass, as per my orders. I turned around to see a small, malicious smile forming on his face.

Suddenly, I felt very, very scared.

After I saw the damages alcohol had on my father, I vowed not to go near it in my life. I had not touched a drop up to this point and suddenly my vulnerability and fear was depending on this glass. So was my life.

"Cheers," he said, raising his glass.

I inhaled tightly, before he and I took a sip of the whisky simultaneously. Whilst he gulped it down smoothly and easily, my throat burned at the sharp tang and my eyes started welling up and I almost started a coughing fit after a single sip.

It made me wonder why people would even want to drink this stuff.

"Another?" He laughed at my reaction. I couldn't tell if he was being serious or not, but he didn't seem to stop me when I refilled both glasses, doing exactly as I was told.

I was scared of him.

He had a gun. He could beat me. He could skin me. He could feed me to the wolves. He had threatened me already anyways. He had the power to do whatever he wanted with me, because I was a prisoner and he wasn't.

So I didn't bother talking back or refuting his orders even after a few rounds. I was dizzy (although he seemed just fine) and scared and so I did exactly as he said, exactly as I was told to.

But then, it changed. He was still on his bed and I was standing patiently by. He had all the power and I had nothing. It was late at night but he didn't seem very tired.

"Now, let's have some fun," he said, staring at me with a mischievous grin. My head was hurting but I could still manage to make out what he was saying. "Take off your dress."

It was like the entire world became still at that precise moment. I felt a tugging at my chest that echoed throughout my body in my intoxicated blood. I felt physically sick, ready to throw up.

"What?" I whispered, though I heard exactly what he had said.

"Take off your dress," he repeated, his tone more cold.

"No, please." I begged, my voice almost breaking, but it was futile. I looked down, feeling queasy.

He sat up properly, leaning against the backboard before he propped his tumbler on the bedside table. Everything he did was measured and it was intimidating. The way he then looked at me was scarring, with fire for eyes and pursed lips, I was petrified about what he was going to do.

"Whilst you're here, you do exactly as you're told, understand?" I nodded my head vigorously, too fearful to protest. "Then I don't see why we should have a problem."

So I did exactly as he said, exactly as I was told to. Without another word, I unbuttoned the dress and pushed it off my shoulders, letting it fall to the floor, leaving me in my stockings and flimsy underwear.

I felt exposed.

Volatile.

Insignificant.

Probably because I was all three.

His eyes raked my almost bare body with precision and comfort, welcoming themselves to peer wherever they wished. I was fighting down streams of tears, trying to be strong but nothing seemed to be working.

"What's the matter?" He asked, taking another sip of the alcohol at hand. When I was silent for a moment, by the look on his face, he didn't seem pleased.

I felt scared.

"I haven't done this before." I managed to croak out.

"You haven't done this before? A girl as pretty as you? That's hard to believe."

It wasn't. I was just waiting for marriage. Mama always told me only my husband deserved my virtue, but here I was, almost bare but a few pieces of fabric in front of a man whose name I did not even know.

"Come here," he said, extending an arm out.

That night, I did exactly as he said, exactly as I was told to.

He made me do things. Things I didn't even know people did.

And when I was certain that he was fast asleep, I clenched my eyes shut as the first tear fell.

•••

Chapter 2

- -

I was sitting in the basement of the house on a stool, a hot water bottle pressed to my lower abdomen, too exhausted to cry.

"You knew he was going to do that to me." My voice was shaking. "Look perfect. You were setting me up."

"Look, it's not my job to question the morals of this house." Matron continued with her work, directing other maids and prisoners in maid uniforms as if I wasn't sitting here at all. Hearing me weep quietly to myself, she sighed. "I just do what I'm told, just like you."

I thought about all the things he made me do. The things he said. The way the song my father and I once danced to was playing softly in the background. The way I laid there next to him for at least an hour, staring blankly at the ceiling before I passed out.

"You could have at least told me he was going to do that."

I thought about the way he looked at me after he finished doing what he did with apathy for eyes, and whispered, "You did well," as if I had accomplished anything.

"Would you have really wanted me to?" I stayed silent.

I thought about the way I limped down the stairs to the basement. The way the pain felt stained on my body. The way I almost tripped several times because my vision was blurred by anger and sadness and agony.

I didn't even know his name.

"Will you at least tell me who he is?" Matron whizzed around with a shocked expression plastered over her face.

"You don't know who he is?" She scowled, disbelievingly. "Oskar Diedrich."

For a short time, she stared at me expecting for something to click in my mind, but nothing came. The name jogged no memory but her tone was sufficient enough to tell me that whatever his name was, he was powerful and I should be scared of him. Witnessing the blank expression on my face, Matron sighed deeply.

"You do know his father, yes? Reichsführer Damien Diedrich?" I shook my head. Matron sighed once more. "Other than the Führer, Goebbels and Göring themselves, there are very few people who outrank him, making him a very dangerous man. He is also the commandant of this camp."

"Reichsführer? Then why is he here and not in Berlin or on the front line?" It was strange to hear a man of such power would offer his time and skills to a largely inert women's camp hidden in the country just out of Berlin. I had been here a month yet I had not heard the supposedly notorious name.

"No one is entirely sure, but there are rumours that they've developed a bomb five times as destructive as any nuclear weapon we know of yet, two miles north of the camp. For the USSR. They say he's here to oversee the manufacturing, which is plausible since the Führer would need someone he trusts. Completely secretive project."

Flooded with knowledge, my head started pounding alongside the ache in the lower half of my body. The number of innocent people it would kill.

"Mind you, I've heard some saying that they're experimenting with some of the women here which explains why some girls go missing every so often. I, myself, have overheard some generals talk of a bomb so powerful, it can shatter bones to dust even if you're miles away from the point of impact, literally!" She swivelled back round and continued with her usual work from where she left off before nonchalantly. "Anyways, I'm just the Matron of the house. It's not my place to pry and you shouldn't either."

"And the son? What is he like?" Though I had already depicted him as a self-important, narcissistic hellion, I was eager to know what Matron would say, seeing as she seemed to know more about him than me. "Oskar, right?"

"Herr Diedrich to you." She scolded. "He is like every boy his age; drinks, smokes, stays out late with his friends. Girls." I winced. "But he cares about his country and his family, making him a better man than you think he is."

That felt like a kick in my stomach.

"No, he's not." I argued, unamused of her tolerance for him. He was a monster. He was vile and sick and he disappointed me as a fellow human being. I could only imagine all the other terrible things he's done. Monster.

"Just because he does bad things doesn't make him a bad person. He's a good kid, but it will always be the tree that makes the apple grow into what it is."

A very rotten apple indeed.

"How can you defend him? You know what he's capable of. You know what he's done." The pain pulsed in my body, causing me to arch forward. Or maybe it was just the weight of my head recovering from intoxication, sleepless and overdosed on shock. "Him just being his father's son doesn't make him a better person."

"Foolish girl," she muttered under her breath, brushing me off. "It's six am now, you may change and get back to the camps. Forget everything you saw here."

Leaving the house held less admiration than when I entered it mere hours ago. The outside no longer seemed majestic or desirable or anything near homely. It felt cold and malicious as it stood spitefully in its great size, coated by high rise forestry. It made me feel sick to my stomach, knowing that I was used under that roof, a roof I did not know existed until tonight. It made me feel sick knowing I was hurt under that roof and every time I tried to scream, it was muffled by trepidation and immobility.

I wanted to run. Run for my life and hide.

But the iron gates and electrified fence topped with barbed wire loops held a different story.

When I returned to the camps, it was just like the beginning of any other busy day, but today I felt different. I felt dirty, though there was not a spot of mud on me yet. I felt exhausted, even though it was just the start of the day.

The area was largely empty, slowly filling with ungroomed women by the minute. Everyone got to their stations like robots - the younger girls would go straight to cleaning and the fit and healthy older ones were sent to do the very laborious work. The older, more fragile women did the cooking and cleaning and every so often, when their arms and legs became too worn out to be of any profitable use, they wouldn't turn up to their posts and a distant gunshot would be the only telltale remnants of their fate.

SS officers were posted sparingly across the camps. I had heard rumours that in co-gendered and male camps, SS men swarmed the area like termites, but that was unknown of here since the women were much more docile.

After my eventful night, I didn't get the opportunity to go back to my cabin to get a blink of sleep, not that I thought I would've anyways. I wanted to find my mother and hold her and tell her what happened. I wanted to cry in her arms and pretend everything was alright. I wanted to braid Lola's mop of hair even if it meant I had to take it out later anyways. I wanted to hold all the pieces of my family I had left and forget about everything from last night, but it was already six thirty and I had to get to work.

I got to my station in a vast vegetation field and picked up my shovel. I got to work straight away, trying to consume my time with labour in attempt to block out all other thoughts.

Impassively, I dug. I was assigned a row and I dug and dug and dug for hours. My arms were numb and sweat mixed with mud coated my face, but I found a ferocity in my body fuelled by anger that I couldn't find a means to stop, just release.

Work at home usually consisted of sewing or cleaning as my feeble physique had never been known to cater well for manual labour. I didn't feel stronger today, though. I had a drive that wouldn't find itself to stop. The ache in my head only diffused into every other cell of my body as I worked harder and harder throughout the day, but I was eager to not pay any attention to it.

By the time it was almost midday, my back was aching and my arms felt as though they were going to fall off, but my mind wasn't bare and barren like I hoped it would be. Images in a reel of torture constantly ran through my head.

Me taking my dress off. Him calling me 'pretty' like it meant anything. His hands unwelcome but still roaming all over my body. At least I could thank the fact that I had not got my period since I was admitted to the camps, preventing any chances of -

In what was a blur, I saw my life flash before my eyes.

I turned around to find a tall, brute officer staring down at me, anger smeared across his face... covered head to toe in dirt.

And I didn't just mean his highly esteemed Blackshirts uniform. A good shovel-full of dark, fertile soil sat chipper on his shoulders, head and the tip of his nose like wondering dust that had settled on a windowsill. I wanted to say that age or illness was the culprit for him being covered head to toe in dirt, but it wasn't. I was.

I had been digging so senselessly that I didn't even realise he was standing behind me the moment I chose to fling a shovel of dirt over my shoulder. My mouth hung open. This is it. This is how I'm going to die.

He gritted his teeth, tightly grabbing hold of my forearm in a vicelike grip that was surely cutting off my blood circulation. If it weren't doing so, I was certain that my heart rate was up beyond humanly possible as he tempestuously tugged me out of the field.

I stumbled several times on the journey but he didn't stop once, dragging me across the scabrous floor, if necessary. He took long, angry strides until we reached an enclosed spot in the midst of the trees, where I was sure no one would find me.

He could shoot me and toss my body to the wolves and no one would know.

The only words that touched my lips were constant prayers, but they weren't helping. He pushed me to the floor in a sharp movement, the jagged stones on the ground cutting through the flimsy material of my skirt and into my knees with a sting. It was now that I realised I was crying, tears flooding down my face in a desperate plea for mercy.

His immense size towered over me, overcasting any light in my sight. I clasped my hands together, begging for any form of sympathy even though I knew better. Men like him were cold and emotionless.

He reached for his gun in practised motion and pressed it against my forehead. The cold metal against my bare skin made my blood curdle with fear and the inability to anticipate my forthcoming death. I closed my eyes tightly, muttering one final prayer.

Three, two, one...

"Put the gun down." I opened one eye to witness the familiar voice approaching with steady footsteps. I wasn't dead.

"Sieg Heil!" The posture of the soil-coated soldier tightened as he caught sight of Oskar Diedrich, extending out his right arm in a customary salute.

"Are you deaf or just plain stupid? I said drop the gun." I looked up to notice that the aforementioned object was still pressed against my forehead, but it was quickly removed as he dropped it to the ground. The man looked tense in his presence. "Now, go back to your post."

I watched intently as the soldier victim to my clumsiness scurried away as per Herr Diedrich's demands, immediately and without question. When Herr Diedrich looked satisfied, he turned to face me on the floor with an amused smirk.

"You on your knees, now that's a pretty sight." I stared at him for a moment, mouth agape with incredulity. I had no response. I was ready to vomit at his vulgarness.

He didn't look nearly as bad as I did after all the drinking. He looked neat and tidy in respectable attire, as if last night didn't happen at all.

"Get up." He gave a small laugh, extending his arm out to me. I furrowed my eyebrows, bemused at the gesture. He just rolled his eyes. "I'm trying to help you, now get up."

So I took his hand and got to my feet, looking everywhere else but at him. I didn't believe he was actually trying to help me, but I was scared about what he would do if I refused. His hand was firm but warm, a feeling that sparked painful memories in my mind.

His hands unwelcome but still roaming all over my body...

"Did you help me because I slept with you?" I mentally slapped myself for verbalising my inner thoughts so bluntly. I couldn't find any other reason for him having saved me since it wasn't as if my death would have affected him at all. If only my mouth didn't speak before my mind did.

"Is that how low you think of me?" Yes. He laughed, evidently entertained by my question. "Of course not. I helped you because you're the first person I've met who actually knows a High Hatters song. I was pleasantly surprised."

"Oh." Taken aback by his response, I could only provide a one syllable answer. Was it all a joke to him? There was no way that knowing a single song had just saved me my life. It was unbelievable.

"What's your name?" His tone was direct and despite his conventional question, it was unnerving.

I didn't like being in his presence. I didn't like the way he looked at me like I was his toy to be humoured by.

"Hana." I mumbled a timid response.

"Okay then, Hana," he plucked a twig from a nearby tree, snapping it in half, "I'll walk you back."

I gulped, halfheartedly trudging behind him as he took lead through the forest. I hugged my chest tightly as the cold bit at my skin, whereas he was impervious to its effect. He walked a few metres upfront, snapping the twig in his hand periodically and throwing a piece at a time into the detritus that skirted the trees.

"Do you have any family here?" He asked, not bothering to look back at me. It was fair to say that I was rather surprised by his question. Why did he care about my family?

"My mother and my sister." I answered, nonetheless, looking down at the floor as we kept walking.

"A sister? How old is she?"

"Six." I briefly responded.

"Really? I have a six year old sister too! Little devil, she is." He turned his head to say to me with a jovial smile, almost making him seem human.

I remembered what Matron said about him being a family person and it made me wonder what he would do if someone did what he did to me to his sister. It was unfair that he was allowed to be warm and affectionate in the day and a drunk assaulter by night and he would face no repercussions. I was the one that suffered.

We didn't talk much for the rest of the short trip. When the camp started emerging in our sight filled with people, the small smile that idly sat on his face at the mention of his sister soon wiped away back to his usual icy expression.

When we got to the fields, I noticed the soldier, now rid of dirt, staring at me with a cold glare. Herr Diedrich returned an intimidating look on my behalf, causing him to turn away. Then, he faced me.

"You're rather pathetic at shovelling, aren't you?" He stated, matter-of-factly.

"It's subject to opinion." I retorted, although I knew very well that shovelling wasn't my forte. That seemed to amuse him.

"Okay," he looked down at me with a smug grin and said in a hushed yet assertive voice, "from tomorrow morning, you'll work for me."

My eyes widened with disbelief. No, no, no, no, no!

There was no way in hell I wanted to work for him. I would rather shovel everyday, all day!

He walked away before I could complain, leaving me stranded with the awful thought of having to see his face and having to be reminded of what he did to me everyday. I couldn't bare it.

I already felt dirty. And used. And worthless. My virtue was ripped out of my hands faster than I could protest and now I was expected to work for the culprit.

That night, when I finally got back to the cabin hoping to get some rest, no sleep came. I clutched onto mama tightly, unable to speak and aching. Her hand combed down my hair consolingly, but the burning sensation in my chest wouldn't ease.

"It's okay, darling, you'll be okay. We'll be okay." She said as my eyes flooded her lap, but for the first time, her words weren't helping.

Her voice sounded strained and suddenly I started feeling incredibly concerned for her health. It wasn't like there much I could do, though. The infirmary here only had the basic facilities and they would kill her if they thought she was unfit to work. I shoved those thoughts aside, well aware of how strong my mama was.

Helplessness started feeling like part of the composition of my blood, running throughout my body in pulses of painful stabs. Tomorrow, that would be put to the test once again and I didn't think I was strong enough to be able to suffer through that once more. I wasn't a strong person like mama. I was fragile and scared and he was happy to take full advantage of that.

"No, I won't." I replied to her, voice cracking, knowing that whatever he had in store for me was not going to be anything short of torture.

Chapter 3

"He usually wakes up at around six, but you have to be here at five. You will help prepare his breakfast, which he eats half an hour after his father at around half past seven, which is when you'll do his bed and tidy his room. Then you'll come down and help tidy up and see if anyone needs help in the kitchen. Understand?"

Overloaded with information by the Matron, I nodded my head, pretending I absorbed all of that. She was walking at an incredibly fast pace around the basement kitchens as I trailed along behind her, attempting to learn my new schedule.

"He doesn't spend much time at home, he's usually in the camps or out with friends. Most of the time he eats lunch elsewhere. If Herr Diedrich chooses to come back for dinner, he will eat an hour after his father at around eight or nine. You'll never find them eating together. In-between that time, you'll clean his room, wash and press his clothes and anything else he tells you to. Hans will inform you on the specifics of the cleaning."

"Why doesn't he eat with his father?" I asked curiously, sure I was told he was a family man just yesterday.

"What did I tell you about prying?" Matron narrowed her eyes at me, warningly. "After dinner, he will either go to his room or go out with his friends. If he stays at home, you'll wait on him until he tells you you're free to leave. If he goes out with his friends, you'll wait for him until he comes back and tells you you're free to leave, which at earliest will be four am."

"Four am? When am I supposed to sleep?" I tried taking in as much as she said, already exhausted by the condense schedule.

"You don't." She replied, snappily. I blinked hard with bafflement. A slender looking, blond haired boy approached us, sporting a ragged striped uniform with a matching hat. He smiled warmly at me with a wave. "Hana, this is Hans. He'll show you what to do from here." With that, the Matron was off in a rush.

"Hi, I'm Hans." He greeted, politely. He looked fairly young even with his slouchy posture, but he had a welcoming look on his face that was a real contrast to Matron's grimace. "Your name's Hana, right? That's so cool! Our names are almost the same. Hans, Hana, get it? Just the last letter that's different. Mines an 's' and yours is an 'a'."

I smiled at his kindness, something I hadn't seen in a man for quite a while. It was refreshing, to say the least.

"You're supposed to tell me the ins and outs of my duty?" I replied, smiling for the first time I had in weeks.

"Oh, yes." He said, gesturing for me to follow him to a cabinet of cleaning goods. "There's not that much to do, really. You have a very lucky job."

By eleven pm, I had changed his bedsheets, ironed his outfits for the upcoming week, scrubbed his floors, dusted absolutely everything and all other domestic chores you could possibly think of.

In all fairness, I was accustomed to it since I would take the heavier bearing of all the housework at home in Berlin whilst mother did the cooking and attended to young Lola and my drunken father. The exhausting part was having to work in a room that only served to induce painful memories of me being violated, still fresh in my memory.

The layout of his room never left my mind. The vinyls, the decanter, the chaise. Even the feeling of his mattress felt imprinted on my body and the images that accompanied those memories sent excruciating shocks down my spine.

But I pushed them out, eager to do my job. Hans was right. I was lucky for him to ask me to be here since my other option was to break my bones a hundred times a day. Cooking and cleaning fit into my skill set, I just had to learn to adjust to the setting. It made me feel better knowing that Herr Diedrich wasn't home very often and also by the fact that I had not seen him all day, to my relief.

At the moment, I was wiping his dressing table. I was behind on schedule but Hans said that was fine for today since I started late anyways. I straightened the various bottles of perfume and other miscellaneous objects, sure not to leave a spec of dust anywhere.

I was rather intrigued to see a single photo frame planted on the table, filled with a black and white picture of Herr Diedrich surrounded by three beautiful girls.

He was sat in the middle in a sleek black suit, looking very debonair, with one girl on his lap and a girl on either side. The tallest and oldest looking girl standing to his right looked about ten in a knee length dress. Her dark hair and facial structure was similar to Herr Diedrich's and even his stony glare was paralleled on her face.

The girl standing to his left was noticeably shorter but still attained the same, distinct facial features wearing the same dress. She looked displeased with her intense gaze through the camera as she stuck her tongue out comically.

The final girl, perched sideways on his lap with his arms circled around her seemed the youngest of them all. She looked around three or four with her large baby eyes and her giddy smile as she rested her head against her brother's chest. She, too, was in a similar dress to the accompanying girls and held a similar jawline and cheek structure to the others. Her hair, however, was noticeably lighter than the other three, but they all seemed to fit in perfectly with each other for the family photo. It almost made my heart melt.

He looked like a regular person, almost. Not the kind of person that would callously kill people or use women at his discretion. He looked younger in the picture, so I was presuming it was taken two or three years ago. It was funny, how sweet and innocent a picture could make a person look. He wasn't innocent at all.

"Hana?" If it weren't for my already tight grip on the meaningful photo frame, I most definitely would have dropped it out of shock.

I stood there, frozen, mouth ajar, as Herr Diedrich presented himself at the doorway. His eyes travelled up from his possession in my hand until they locked on my own eyes, sending me shivers. It was safe to say I was very prepared to melt into oblivion at that moment.

I was shaking internally but outside, I was too paralysed to move an inch. I watched as he approached me slowly with confident strides until he was right behind me. His firm chest was pressed against my back, leaving me unable to move.

"It's a funny pattern, isn't it." His arm came forward, taking the photo frame out of my hand. "You," he whispered in my ear as he stuffed the picture into one of the drawers, "in my room," his hand swiftly moved the hair from my right shoulder to one side, exposing my neck, "touching things you shouldn't be."

I let out a small gasp as his arm snaked around my waist whilst his lips came in contact with my neck. He left a soft trail of kisses from the crook of my neck downwards, pushing the sleeve of my dress off my shoulder to give him more access. As I tried to flinch away, his arm around my waist tightened, pressing me against him harder.

Eventually, I just let him. Not because I wanted him to or because I was enjoying it, but because I was merely a nobody. I was his prisoner. Not his guest, nor his friend or his wife. I was his property and he could do whatever he wanted with me and I didn't have the right to protest.

The feeling of his body pressed against mine almost made bile rise up my throat. It only reminded me of the events of two nights ago, a night I was finding difficult to bleach out of my memory.

It came to me as quite a surprise when his lips detached from my skin and he pulled me round to face him. I knew he probably had something up his sleeve. If he was going to hurt me again, I wasn't going to be naive about it this time.

His face was mere inches away from mine. For a split second, I thought I could see the boy from the picture I was holding a minute ago, but it quickly flashed back to the unfeeling man standing before me.

"I could use you again, right now. This very moment." There it was. I gnawed on the inside of my cheeks at his perilous words, my arms trembling. "But I'm not going to."

He stepped away, unhurriedly making his way to his bed where he sat down, eyes fixated on me. Nervousness was pouring out of my every orifice as I stood there, shaking, anticipating what he would do next.

"And I don't know if it's because of your undeniably good music taste or the fact that you have actually done a rather good job of cleaning my room, but either way, consider yourself safe."

I looked around, stunned by the fact he commended my work. That wasn't a necessity nor did I think he would have considered it a courtesy. In all honesty, I didn't think he would have even noticed that I had cleaned his room at all considering how privileged he was. Moreover, the butterflies in my stomach settled knowing that he wasn't planning to have me take my dress off again; a grand relief.

From his bed, he looked at me up and down with an eyebrow raised. His eyes wondered from my legs up to my chest. I quickly crossed my arms, feeling exposed under his heavy stare. Once again, queasiness boiled in my stomach as I stood there, unsure of what to do.

"Why aren't you wearing the correct uniform?" He asked, catching me off guard. I looked down at my attire; a spare dress Hans had retrieved for me that was meant for the cooking staff, not maid-wear.

"Matron said she didn't have the time to sew my triangle onto a maid outfit and that it was more essential to have the correct badge. I'll have it by tomorrow, though." I explained, doing my best to string the words together fluidly. With his daggers for eyes targeted at me, my speech was broken up and didn't sound half as fluent as I hoped.

I gulped as he rose from his bed and made his way over to me. He didn't look pleased at all as his fingers started outlining the plain red triangle sewed onto the chest of my dress. I shivered under his touch and my airway felt suddenly blocked.

"I don't want you to wear it. I'll inform Matron. Make sure you wear the correct uniform tomorrow." His expression exuded ice.

He knew his power, he knew his control. He was the kind of cold that would make you rethink the idiosyncrasy of our Arctic and Antarctic knowledge and you could see it from the moment you saw the blue of his eyes. But, here, right now, I noticed a little idiosyncrasy of his that got me out of a second night of being used and it was his profound love of music, mirrored in myself. Also, like me, he had a deep love for his sisters like any ordinary person, not an idiosyncrasy at all.

But the moment you would think that there is something solemn in him (like when you're holding a photo frame or when he stops you from being shot), he will look at you with an impassive stare and almighty stance and once again you were greeted by the self-righteous soldier that blurred the line between morality and immorality with his own two feet and gun-filled hand.

"Why not?" I asked, since by any other regulation, wearing the triangle was a must, only alleviated by his direct demands.

"It's disgusting. I don't want to see it in my room everyday." He looked at me like I was horrific and vile for the single colour stamped on my dress. "Anyways, I don't have to explain myself to you. Just do as you're told."

He wore the swastika with so much pride, the corruption of the symbol parallel to his disposition. Here he was, abhorred by the symbol my chest bares because I was the one punished for trying to help others but he was awarded medals and notoriety for putting a bullet in helpless people's heads.

"I didn't do anything wrong." I argued, slightly proud of my newfound bravery but more so terrified by how he would react. He scoffed and looked at me as if I was scum on the sole of his shoe.

"Let me tell you something, Hana." My name on his lips made my intestines twist, intimidated by the disdain he had for me. "The red symbolises that you've got really deranged opinions and you fall for bullshit like, say, Communism, which is bad enough in itself, but you know what's worse than just being a political prisoner?"

I didn't nod or shake my head or mutter a breath. His candid words were striking, hitting my skin harder than any stone or knife. I gulped as the sound of blood rushing to my ears filled my senses. His hand found its way under my chin, a gentle finger lifting up my face so my eyes were on his.

"The fact that it's a plain, red triangle. Nothing more. You know what this means? It means not only are you a criminal, but you're also a traitor. Your loyalties weren't with your country how it was supposed to be and that's worse than being Jewish or Polish or Russian or anything else." He chucked, smugly. "How does that feel, Hana?"

My father died, protecting my mother from the same fate. Neither him nor her nor I had done anything to ever disgrace our country. I loved Germany. We loved Germany. It was our home and the only home we knew. He was trying to get under my skin and he succeeded.

"I'm not a criminal!" I bellowed, though my voice came out more timid than I sounded in my head. He was amused by my outburst, circling around me like I was a stray animal lost in direction.

"Then what are you? Other than a disgrace to Germany? It sickens me that people like you call yourself German."

I was angry. Fists formed at my side, my nails drawing blood as they dug into the palm of my hands. Mind clouded with rage, I was prepared to leap at him if I didn't lack the physical strength to do so. Son of a -

"I'm more German than you'll ever be!"

The slap struck me so fast I barely saw it coming. I stumbled back and steadied myself on his table, head dizzy at the impact. His hand hit my face so fiercely that I could feel its sting reverberate throughout the rest of my head and pricked tears in my eyes. My hand quickly went to cradle my cheek, which was starting to become numb with pain.

I had crossed the line with what I said and we both knew it.

"I admire you standing up for your nationality, but I won't tolerate you questioning my integrity. Understand?" His tone was cold and petrifying as he looked down at me with a composed posture.

I nodded immediately, not daring to speak back to him again, not daring to speak at all.

"Good. You may leave. Ensure you are provided with the appropriate uniform for tomorrow."

Recollecting my stability with one hand still pressed against my burning face, I set forth for the door, impatient to leave.

"Oh, and Hana," he called. I stopped at the doorway with my head down, on the verge of crying. "Well done for today. There should be some bread on the dining table. Take some for your family and make sure no one sees you."

I was aching to stab him but I also didn't want the burden of taking a life on my hands.

He didn't want to help me. He used me. He demeaned me. He slapped me. And the next moment he would pretend he cared by offering me food or stopping me from being killed, as if having the same music taste was somehow my saving grace. I was merely a puppet to his pathetically cruel games and I was forsaken in the matter.

I shut the door behind me and left with no response, a hand shielding the throbbing side of my face from anyone seeing it. I went downstairs to the lavish dining room and saw, as described, an arrangement of bread on the side table. I hastily stuffed two rolls into my pocket as he offered, cautious of anyone passing by. Heading for the back door, a familiar voice stopped me in my tracks.

"Hana, your face! It looks awful!" Hans remarked, eyes gauged open at me. "No, wait, I didn't mean it like that, your face is very beautiful, it's just-" Realising what he just said, his eyes widened even more. I was just utterly confused. "Never mind. Please, let me get you an ice pack."

"That's really not necessary, Hans. I really need to get back to the camp." I replied, impatient to get as far away from here as possible.

"What happened, Hana?" He sounded solemn and it felt somewhat affectionate, especially after he had just accidentally called me beautiful.

"Please don't tell anyone you saw me, Hans."

"Hana, wait!" I felt awful as I evaded his question and moved for the door, trying to cover up my possibly bruised face.

I walked at a fast pace through the dimly lit, fenced path connecting the house to the camps. Flickering overhead lamps offered some guidance as it lighted the narrow road, guarded by motionless soldiers standing equal intervals apart.

The brute house glowed out in the darkness with its lamps and the faint glow of the illuminated rooms through the window, but the frosty autumn night held more warmth than that building ever could.

It was barren, yet brimming with illicit activities and immorality; a hell-house guarded by the arms of lurching trees and prided flags of see-through Nationalism.

Deceptively drawing, you would never imagine the kind of illegalities that took place in there.

Entering cabin 14, the poignant stench of sweat and decay pervaded my nostrils. The women were visibly exhausted, cramped into their respective bunks like cattle in a farm; a disconcerting image. It was fairly quiet as most women were trying to gain as much sleep as possible in the short timeframe, but little mumbles of mothers' prayers and children's weeps were still audible.

Tenderness welled in my heart as I saw Mama curled up on a mattress with Lola's arms around her. Their faces beamed as they saw me approach them, welcoming me with a warm embrace.

"I missed you." Lola pressed a fat kiss on my cheek, a hand slyly slipping into my dress pocket to pull out a bread roll. "Is this for me?" She sang with a cheeky grin and I nodded in response.

"But you can't tell anyone we have it, alright?" Mama gave me a confused look but I reassured her everything was fine. She looked weak and tired, much like all the other hardworking women here.

I fed the second roll to Mama bit by bit, only taking pinches for myself. Lola had one for herself, hiding it under her blouse to be extra careful no one else saw.

The bread they served in the camps was stale and unappetising, barely enough to energise one for a hard day of labour. Part of me felt awful as we three ate as everyone else was dreaming of decent food, but I was just as helpless as them in the matter. I had to ensure Mama and Lola were okay first.

Lola had almost finished her piece as she sat up to press her mop of chocolate hair against my arm. "What happened to your face? Did you steal the food?"

"No, she didn't. Did you?" Mama questioned, looking at me very concerned. Before I could mutter a response, Mama sat up and started coughing hysterically, leaving me incredibly distressed.

I rubbed her back, thinking maybe she just got some bread stuck in her throat, but all my worries amplified into a plethora of fear as her hand retracted from her mouth, covered in blood.

•••

A/N

First days on the job never really go well, now do they?

What do you think of the story so far, and what do you think will happen next?

Thank you so much for reading and I love reading all your comments I hope you enjoyed this chapter.

Chapter 4

A long night pursued after witnessing my mother almost suffocate and bleed to death, but it warranted no sufficient excuse to not show up to work at five am the following morning.

The day passed fairly the same as yesterday, only today I had to bear the weight of knowing Mama was lying alone in the infirmary without me or Lola or decent medical attention by her side. Drowned in mop buckets, floor cleaner and a steam-swamped kitchen, the effort of keeping my mind off Mama's condition didn't go to full waste. I was even graced by the charm of not having to see Herr Diedrich at all today and now I was just waiting for him to return so I could be dismissed and go see my mother.

I stood patiently in his room (careful not to pick up anything I shouldn't, from experience), awaiting his return. An hour passed, then two, until it reached midnight and the aching desire to see my mother was eating out at me. I couldn't leave until he let me but it didn't look like he was coming back anytime soon, since Matron stated four am earliest. Maybe if I explained to her my circumstance, Matron would let me go on her authority. I had to make sure Mama was stable and I was hoping that meant more to her than it does to him.

I stepped out of his room, adrenaline kicking in as my heartbeat rose to my ears. I checked left and right, ensuring not many people were around, reassured by the fact it was past midnight so most workers would be resting in the camps or working down in the basement. I tiptoed down the grand staircase and every step I took told me that this was a bad idea.

Maybe I should just go back. Even if he returned at four, at least I could see my mother with my mind more at ease.

It was that moment where I was enriched by the presence of Herr Diedrich stumbling in through the door, a bottle in one hand and a darkening bruise on the other.

My eyes travelled up to his face, decorated with a bruised jaw and a nasty gash on his forehead that left a trail of blood down his cheek. His dreary eyes lit up when they landed on me, instantly staggering over in my direction.

I didn't know what to do. Maybe he was drunk enough to not realise if I ran away? I could pretend I'm someone else and just casually walk by?

Sighing, I walked over to him and pulled his arm around my shoulders for support.

My inner voice told me that he deserved to suffer considering the countless lives he has taken. He was a ruthless soldier and a depraved person. Thousands like me were trapped under his sort of terror and I could only imagine how much that was going to inflate by over the war. Even if it meant I couldn't kill him myself, what harm could it do to leave him to bleed for just one night?

My conscience started kicking in, screaming don't you dare. What kind of person have I become? The girl I was three days ago would never leave a person to sit in pain no matter what their crimes. Who was I to decide what kind of punishment each person deserves?

Anyways, if he did end up bleeding to death, I would have to go back to shovelling the watchful eye of dozens of gun armed and life mouldering SS men, which didn't seem very attractive at all.

"Careful," I advised, guiding his weight on me up the stairs attempting to not fall. He tripped and toppled, tightening his grip around me for constant balance. He winced as I grabbed his injured hand to level his weight on my shoulders.

The stench of alcohol was prominent on him as Herr Diedrich took another swing of the liquid in his hand. Slipping the bottle away from him, a resentful expression replaced his drunken scowl.

"M-mine!" He lunged for the bottle, stumbling and falling head first onto the sharp edge of a step, pulling me down with him.

I managed to minimise the impact on me by extending my arms out in front, leading only to a sharp hit on my forearm and not my face. However, he was not wise (or sober) enough to do the same, causing the already heavy cut on his forehead to deepen even more.

"Ow!" He shrieked, pressing a hand against his forehead only for it to come away covered in blood.

That reminded me, I had to get back to see my mother.

But I couldn't just leave him here either and there didn't seem to be any one else walking by. How convenient.

Resentfully, I managed to get him back up again with all my strength and none of his effort and proceeded to pull him into his room. I set him down on his bed before running into his en suite to retrieve the first aid kit.

I was glad to see it was fully stocked and didn't solely comprise of cheap tissues and two plasters like our first aid box did at home. I pulled out the necessary items and started cleaning the awful mess on his forehead as he sat benignly on the end of his bed. Occasionally, he would jerk away at the sting of the antiseptic, like a little baby, but I gently held his chin until his face was clean. I was glad that it wasn't deep enough to need stitches and he could get away with just a plaster. He eyed the bottle I left on his bedside table wistfully and then looked back at me with pleading eyes.

"No more of that for you tonight, mister." I insisted gently, earning a disappointed frown from him. The smell of antiseptic started drowning away the foul stench of whatever he was drinking, calming to my senses. Plastering it up, I then focussed my attention to his bruising jaw and hand. "I'll be back in a moment, don't go anywhere."

I ran down to the basement kitchen and grabbed two packs of frozen peas. Thankfully, it was busy enough for no one to bother questioning my intentions, allowing me to go in and out fairly quickly. When I returned with the stated items, he looked at me bizarrely.

"I'm not hungry." He sulked, turning his face away from me. Ignoring his drunken behaviour, I crouched before him and pressed a pack to his jaw and and lifted his uninjured hand up to it to replace mine, before pressing the other against his bruised hand. "I hate peas." He stated, sullenly.

"Did you get into a fight?" I asked, although I knew I shouldn't have. I was poking for information that was none of my business. My only business on which my life depended on was making sure Herr Diedrich was attended to and nothing more. It came as a surprise to me when he nodded and didn't defer away from my question like I thought he would. "Did you start it?"

"I threw the first punch, but I didn't start it." I knew he was telling the truth by the way his eyes flickered towards me and by the way his grip on the frozen peas tightened. I was expecting him to leave it at that, but he continued. "Son of a bitch called my mother a whore. Nobody speaks about my mother like that."

Without realising, a small smile tugged at my lips. I knew he was a person who deferred to violence and used violence as a physic outlet but it only made his affection for his mother stand out more. If I had the comparable physical strength, I most definitely would have done the same thing if it meant defending my mother, so who was I to judge?

I was taken aback when his soft touch lifted up my chin to look directly at him. I was still crouched in front of him with my hand on top of his, only a pack of peas between us. He gazed at me intensely as his thumb tenderly brushed against my cheekbone down to my jaw, leaving a small burning sensation in its path.

"I didn't mean to hit you yesterday, Hana." He retracted his hand as if he had stung himself by touching me. Looking down, he muttered, "It was an accident. I'm so sorry."

"An accident? What, your hand has a mind of its own now?" I teased, amused by his drunken persona. He nodded fervently like a child trying to get himself out of trouble. Deep down, I was warmed by his apology, something I never expected.

"Oh really? And I'm just expected to forgive you? Why don't you prove it?" I immediately started regretting what I said as a devilish smirk appeared on his face.

"If you take your clothes off and get in my bed, I will." I couldn't help myself but laugh at his playful words.

But then it quickly went away. The images of my bare body in his bed stormed back into my memory. My smile faltered. Remember who he is, Hana. He's not a good person.

"May I leave?" I asked, my throat tightening. I needed to get to the infirmary.

"Do you have to?" The strain in his voice caused a tugging at my chest. He faced away from me with a look of despair as he took his shoes off and lied down on his bed. In what was almost a whisper, he said, "Please don't go."

It was enlightening to see him so... vulnerable. His spasms of being human played with my head but it was such a subliminally intriguing game. One moment I was staring daggers at the machine that didn't contain any sense of morals but the next I was watching a hurt child tucking himself into bed, yearning not to be alone.

"Okay." Taking a deep breath, I crawled into his bed next to him, greeted by an arm wrapped around my waist. I revelled in his warmth and the coziness of his duvet, a luxury I had missed for a long time.

I blocked out the lurid memories of being in this bed with the constant concern for Mama and I did my best to block those thoughts out for the night by trying to relax and get a decent nights sleep.

-

Remember when I said that at times he could extraordinarily be a decent person from time to time?

I take that back.

"Hana, what are you doing here?" He said, voice rough. Herr Diedrich pressed his hand to his forehead and clenched his eyes shut with the pain of both the alcohol and the injury on his forehead. When his fingers found the plaster, he was visibly displeased. "Who on earth put a plaster on my forehead? Do I look five?"

"No, but you did look severely hurt and bleeding." I explained, but he ignored me completely as he ripped it off before he gradually got up and walked into his bathroom, slamming the door shut.

He clearly did not remember a wink of last night.

But no, that was not why I was infuriatingly mad at him. I didn't need or want his affirmation in any sense.

When he got out of the shower dressed for the day and I had gotten ready in his room (also preparing an excuse as to why I wasn't helping to prepare breakfast in the morning for Matron), he left the room at a hurried pace as if I wasn't there at all.

That was perfectly fine, all until I looked at the clock.

Seven o'clock.

And he was leaving for breakfast.

"Herr Diedrich! Wait!" I called out after him, only resulting in him covering his ears with his hands as he continued to walk away.

"Shut up, Hana. I'm hungover and you screaming like a fish monger isn't helping." He started to walk faster but slowed down again after stumbling a bit. I ran after him, knowing God had left me to ensure all hell did not ensue.

"Wait, please!"

"Hana, shut up and go away. I'm starving. Give me some peace." His hands tightened around his ears as he made his way to the dining room, completely oblivious to the time.

Dear God, We are already suffering in the midst of a horrific war. Please spare me from witnessing another. Please.

"What the hell happened to you?" Reichsführer Diedrich asked from the end of the dining table, referring to the awful condition of Herr Diedrich's face.

I realised that this was the first time I had come across Herr Diedrich's infamous father and the first thought that came into my mind was how eerily similar he looked to Herr Diedrich. The dark hair, the composed posture, the dangerous look in his eye. His uniform was undeniably dignified, complementing his almighty demeanour. His eyes were scanning through the daily paper with a cup of coffee in his hand, indisputably surprised to see his son.

"A situation arose." Herr Diedrich answered curtly, mouth agape as I watched from the doorway. His eyes flicked to the clock and then back at me with a sharp glare, goosebumps arising on my skin with fear.

"And did you diffuse it?" Reichsführer asked with an air of authority, returning his eyes to the paper.

"The matter has been taken care of, yes." Herr Diedrich was rigid. His arms were behind his ramrod straight back as he watched his father carefully. "I should leave."

As he was about to turn and leave, Reichsführer stopped him.

"No, sit. Have a drink." He spoke in such a collected and unobtrusive manner that his words were made imperative before he even muttered them, even to his own son. Herr Diedrich gave me another hateful look as he went to sit down on the opposite end of the table.

I went over to the side table to collect the teapot and then to Herr Diedrich to fill his teacup. His eyes were on me as I filled it up in silence, trying to avoid his uncomfortable stare.

"Ouch!" I hissed, my foot on fire. His foot had landed on mine under the table with a great force, causing me to spill some of the scorching hot liquid on my hand. I bit my lip hard, thinking of everything else in the world but the pain that was searing through my body, aware of Reichsführer's watchful eye. I limped back to the doorway, trying to be as quiet and unnoticeable as possible.

Today I had the pleasure of learning that soldiers do not wear soft slippers around the house but in fact wear very hard and very painful boots that has most definitely crippled my foot. Tea is also very hot and very dangerous as well and should never come in direct contact with your skin.

"So, son. When was the last time you were in the camps?" Reichsführer Diedrich asked, taking a small bite out of his biscuit and putting his paper down.

"Three days ago." Herr Diedrich answered, looking intently down at his beverage. Three days ago, when he stopped me from being shot.

"I insist you go today. I want you to monitor the camps more often, especially since I'm very occupied now with other things." He was stern.

"I can't today. I'm busy." Herr Diedrich replied, his tone clipped and annoyed.

"What can be more important than serving your country, Oskar? Enlighten me." He took a bizarrely patronising sip of his coffee.

"Fine. I'll go now." With that, Herr Diedrich was up and out of the room with great speed, pulling me along behind him. He was stopped midway.

"Remember what I taught you?" Reichsführer asked, setting his paper down on the table.

"Harsh discipline, I know."

Their interactions were cold and minimal, as if they would rather not talk to each other at all. No wonder they are strictly on different timetables.

When we were out of Herr Diedrich's father's earshot, his hands cupped around my face as he started shaking my head hysterically.

"You useless, moronic imbecile! You exasperating bonehead of an inconvenience!"

"Ouch! Ow!" I whined as he flicked my forehead and pulled my ear. My hand and foot was still hurting from the incident mere minutes ago.

"What, that hurts? You pathetic waste of space! You had one job and all it required was you checking the time, you absolute ignoramus!" I frowned, recalling the fifty other jobs I have to do on an hourly basis. "You know what, prepare for a day of living hell!"

My day of living hell started just as we were about to leave the house to head for the camps.

"Hana, I've suddenly forgotten how to do my laces." He said, condescendingly. I looked at him with narrow eyes but he just glared back at me expectingly.

"Your laces are already done." I observed.

"Yes, but they're too loose. Do them again."

Gritting my teeth, I got down on the floor by his feet and redid the laces of his left shoe. As I was about to move on to his right one, he moved away as his attention was directed elsewhere, kicking my face in the process. I held my nose as I started seeing stars.

"Oskar," I heard Matron, who was bearing a smile (something I thought I would never say). "Is there anything I can help you with?"

"Actually there is." He turned to me with an unfulfilled look. "Hana, are you done there?" Resentfully, I crawled over to him and started redoing his other shoelace, well aware of the charming smirk implanted on Matron's face. "I need someone to take over Hana's duty for the morning. We're going out for a walk."

Matron looked down at me cautiously as I stood up and then back at Herr Diedrich. "That can be arranged."

We travelled to the camps through the main path, which I was prohibited to use on a regular basis without the accompaniment of Herr Diedrich. When we got there, each and every soldier saluted Herr Diedrich with the utmost attentiveness, only to receive a very apathetic response.

It was then when I saw the masses of dispirited and colourless women, I realised that I had not seen my mother yet. Guilt churned in my stomach.

"May I use the bathroom please, Herr Diedrich?" I asked in an appallingly sweet tone, desperate to hold Mama.

"No," was his blunt response as he made his way to the front of the possession sorting station with me trailing behind him.

Instead of fighting his demands, I viewed the amassed prisoners slaving away by the rows of tables. All uniformed in ragged blouses and battered skirts, hair unwashed for weeks and hands covered in filth. They worked in silence under the beady eye of Herr Diedrich, not daring to look up or move an inch out of position. Several SS men stood around the area, ready to pounce at anyone who diverted away from their allocated job.

I received some hostile stares as I stood by him silently, no actual job to do. I found that this place fell into the back of my mind, overtaken by a majestic house full of fancy dinnerware and diamonds. It was like I had temporarily forgotten about the women being beaten here and being weakened by the minute. Innocent women. Children. Girls whose only crime was believing in a better Germany.

It was like I had completely forgotten I was one of them.

An hour passed of standing behind Herr Diedrich in silence as he monitored the workings of the section. At one point, he caught a girl slipping some spare food from the luggage of a newcomer into her dress pocket and told a soldier to "Deal with her" and nothing else, before she was torn away and the faint sound of a bullet was heard from the distance.

I gulped, intaking the fresh smell of death and angst as all the women sharpened their pace. The girl looked innocent. Who could she harm with a small bit of food? It might not have even been for herself. Maybe she had family or friends here who needed it more than her but now she was gone to never be seen again.

That could have been me the other day.

I didn't say anything. I didn't question why he let that happen because I already knew. He was a soldier and he would say it's his duty. He didn't care if women like us were killed, what were we to him anyways?

Time dragged by as I stood there uncomfortably, watching my own kind work their backs off as I was shadowing Herr Diedrich. When another two hours passed and the women started faltering in their pace, Herr Diedrich looked displeased and turned to me.

"Tell them to work faster or they will be beaten." He ordered, austerely.

I looked from him to the tired women who still had hours of a days work left. I shook my head, knowing I couldn't do something like that.

"Why can't you do it?" I asked, receiving a disconcerting look from him.

"Because, Hana, I'm still hungover and am not in the mood to shout. It's your fault we're here. You shouldn't be questioning my orders either, unless you want to end up back here."

I was one of them. I slept in the same cabin as some of the girls and I ate the same food as them. But I wanted to say that I also bore the same assorting symbol on my chest and wore the same uniform, but I didn't anymore.

The work I did now was a job the women here would dream of. I no longer had a gun pressed to my head every thirty seconds and I no longer had to freeze in the biting cold and I had done nothing well in particular to deserve it.

"Do it and I won't go harsh on you for the rest of the day." He bargained, but it didn't matter. I didn't have the authority to threaten my fellow prisoners and I didn't have the backbone to do it either. They were meant to be my peers, not the women I threaten. I just couldn't do it. "Fine."

He turned to the man on his left and ordered him to do the same and he readily complied. The fear on the faces of the women was unsettling and the urge to hug my mother was roaring again.

The pace of the sorters didn't slow down again after that and an hour after the incident, Herr Diedrich became bored and no longer wanted to stay in the camps, so he left with me following behind him.

It came as a surprise when he decided to go back into his home which I was informed he never does until nightfall. His father was not home, so he had the time of his life disarranging the entire house to have me clean up after him, periodically poking fun at me and Communists, even though I wasn't one.

The day also passed with a series of 'Hana, get this' and 'Hana, get that,' which, as easy as it sounds, is rather difficult in a house as large as his. It was even more infuriating that he not once used, ate or drank anything he made me retrieve, solely to pull at my strings and whenever I did get him any food, he would top it off with a "Do they serve this in the camps? It's a real shame if they don't," well aware I had not eaten in almost a day and the only food we got was water for soup.

When it reached one am and I had orange juice thrown on me, had my entire life mocked and was exhausted from so much cleaning, I started running out of patience. I was fine with the cleaning and I had grown accustomed to the constant belittling, but I couldn't take the fact that I knew my mother was suffering and I wasn't by her side.

He was lying in his bed, 'reading' a book with a song playing softly in the background (not legal, of course), pelting me with grapes as I scrubbed his floors for the sixth time today, trying to get the orange juice off again.

"Having fun there?" He laughed sadistically but I ignored his comments, as I had been for hours now.

"Herr Diedrich, please may I leave now?" I asked, practically begging. I knew he was punishing me but I didn't know for how long more. I couldn't stay the night again. I had to see Mama.

"Stop talking. Keep cleaning."

"Please. I'm begging you." I lost my dignity the day I was brought here, but I hadn't lost my mother yet and I wasn't going to compromise that now. "Punish me tomorrow. Beat me, use me, whatever you want. Please just let me go for today."

He studied me closely as I stood up from the floor, worry present on my face as I realised I had not seen my mother in almost two days. He was merciless. What made me think he would say yes when he was mad at me for leaving him to eat breakfast with his father?

"Tell me the truth and I will." Hope filled me as I listened to him intently. "Where do you need to go?"

I hesitated for a second, knowing he didn't care about my mother's condition. It probably wouldn't be enough to persuade him, but he would only be angrier if I lied. I looked down and started playing with my fingers, unsure of what to say.

"My mother. She's, umm, sick and I haven't seen her for a while." That was the first time I actually vocalised that, as timid as it was, and I immediately wanted to crawl into a ball.

To my surprise, his face dropped. "Hana, why didn't you tell me?"

I looked up at him, dumbfounded by his earnest reaction. He didn't care, surely. He had never even seen my mother, for crying out loud.

"Why are you just standing there? Leave!" I ran out the door and didn't bother questioning why he let me go like that, more concerned about how my mother was doing.

She was well, I knew it for sure. If anything had happened to her, I would have sensed it in my bones. She was sick once, when I was eight, and I had a feeling in my gut that she was when I was at school. She didn't get sick very often but when she did, she always recovered well because she would fight the illness off herself with her innate strength and valour I had not had the luck to inherit.

When I got to the door of the infirmary, I was greeted by a restless Lola who threw herself at me in a tight hug.

"You said you'd come yesterday." She whined, rubbing the tip of her nose against mine in our traditional Eskimo kiss. Almost seven, she was growing in height faster than I imagined, even on minimal nutrition.

"I'm sorry, Lola." It was a blessing on her that she was still quite oblivious to everything going on around her. The war, the camps, the killings. The naive girl before me was immune to the suffering around her and I prayed she would stay that way for a long time to come.

"Did someone hurt you?" She asked, holding up my partially burnt hand. It hurt less now after I managed to put it in some cold water when I told Herr Diedrich I was going to fill up my mop bucket, but in all honesty I had completely forgotten about it with all the chaos in my head about the woman who raised me.

"No, that's just me being clumsy." I insisted, holding her tighter. I missed her. I missed all the games we would play under a candlelight at night before getting in trouble for not being asleep. I missed teaching her how to read and write and seeing her cry when I told her she spelt a word wrong. "Where's Mama?"

"Frau Schmitz said she's sleeping but she's been sleeping for so long."

Horror.

Horror was the first feeling I felt. It pervaded every bone and cell of my existence, slamming against my skin whilst trapped inside its shell. It infused its harrowing hands into every twist and turn of my mind, squeezing it viciously until all that was left was a puddle of confusion and an ocean of regret.

Regret.

When the horror subdued, or enough to be overtaken, regret drowned me in its ocean of misery. It didn't slam or bash or hit. It slithered around in my stomach and my mind stealthily before it wrapped around my heart and the python of regret constricted its venomous tail around the organs of my existence until all that was left was the shadow of mourning.

Chapter 5

"Is Mama going to come back soon?" Lola asked, hope glistening in her eyes as she cuddled me tightly.

"I... I don't know." My voice was breaking as I pulled her closer to me, resting my chin on her head.

I was ten when she was born and I leaped with joy at the news of a sister. Being an only child was lonely, especially in an inner city area where great grasslands to play with friends were practically nonexistent. She was all the family I had left.

Here I was, now, having to lie to her because I was too scared to overtake the role of her mother, our mother, knowing I could never live up to her. She made me feel safe even when our hands were in shackles and we were watching our house be torn to pieces. She made me feel assured everything would be fine after witnessing my drunk father being shot in the head in our very kitchen.

Now, I couldn't even convince myself that we were going to be remotely okay.

When the alarms rang to commence the day, I went straight to work cutting vegetables after telling Lola that she should not worry about Mama. Right now, I couldn't bear how she would react to the news that the woman we both looked up to died in excruciating pain with one nurse by her side with only weak painkillers to offer.

The kitchen was quiet, contrary to the usual morning buzz, since both Herr Diedrich and his father were out. Alone in the silence, I was overwhelmed by the overflowing anger and resentment in my system.

Anger and resentment at myself.

I should have been with Mama. Even if her death was inevitable, I should have been by her side through every moment of the pain. I should have been there to convince her she would be alright like she had done for me countless times.

But I let her down.

Instead, I was with the man who spent a night defacing my virtue and insulting my identity. An entire night, I laid peacefully by him, telling myself he was vulnerable just like me.

I felt guilty.

It wasn't even him to blame. He was drunk and angry and although it was just a small chink in his armour, I perceived it at a greater magnitude and let myself be fooled by his alter ego. Guilt swarmed the hollow of my heart, poisoning my tears and weakening my bones.

I slept in his arms and convinced myself to feel comfortable there because my mother was too sick to make me feel the same.

He hurt me. He hurt me in multiple ways. But I stayed with him knowing my mother was in pain. How could I have done that?

"He raped me." I whispered into the empty air.

I felt a stab in my chest as I said it out loud for the first time. He raped me. He said I was not German and I spent the night sleeping in his bed because he said sorry. I was pathetic.

"Who?" I jumped as Hans appeared at the doorway, accidentally cutting my head with the knife in the process. I hiss at the sudden sting. I turned to face him, shocked, the same look mirrored on his face.

"Hans, I didn't see you there." Noticing the cut was deep, I wrapped a dishcloth tightly around my hand in attempt to stop the bleeding.

"Who hurt you, Hana? Herr Diedrich?" I hesitated. I was shaking. He picked up on both. "Look, I'm sorry for what he did to you but you can't tell anyone. If anyone finds out, Herr Diedrich will kill you. He's untouchable."

He looked at me solemnly. I was too anxious to tell anyone what happened knowing this is exactly how I would react. I really did not want anyone to know.

However, Hans realised how uneasy I felt and dropped the subject. Instead, he walked over to me with a look of concern and he took my injured hand in his.

"You really are clumsy." Unwrapping the loose dishcloth from my hand, he set it on the counter and guided my hand to under the cold water tap. His hand was cold and soft, rubbing off the drying blood as it oozed out of the cut and trickled down my arm.

Like in an instant, all I could think about was how I helped clean his wounds. Herr Diedrich did not even remember the following morning. Instead, he was annoyed that I had put a plaster on him and was confused why I was even in his bed. The night was a waste and nothing good came out of it, only making the guilt in my veins surge with even more vehemence.

Hans tightly wrapped a bandage around my hand as the bleeding calmed down and bent down to kiss my palm. I was slightly taken aback by the unexpected gesture but he just looked up at me with a smile.

"Thank you." I muttered, dropping my arm to my side rashly. God, do I know how to make things awkward.

"This is probably really bad timing." He let out a nervous laugh. "Herr Diedrich wants to see you."

"What? But I thought he wasn't home."

"He came back a little while ago and asked if you were here. He looked annoyed when I said you were."

My hands formed fists at my side, but quickly relax as I felt the sting of my fresh cut at the pressure. He couldn't still be mad at me about making him drink a cup of tea with his father, could he? I made one mistake. One! He was blowing it way out of proportion.

"Okay, I'll go now."

I knocked on his office door twice, not eager to see him in any respect. What I did want to see was Mama, alive and well and dancing around in our kitchen like she used to.

"Come in." I entered his study to see him on his desk, scribbling away on something that seemed rather important. Closing the door behind me, I waited patiently as he finished the page he was on. The bruises on his face and knuckles didn't seem to be fading but the gash on his forehead was closing quite well. His eyes travelled to my injured hand. "What happened?"

"Accident." I gave a short response, unsettled in his company.

"Why are you here?" He set his pen down on the table as he looked up at me, discontented by my presence.

"You... you asked to see me." I replied, hands behind my back as I did my best to avoid eye contact. "I'm sorry about yesterday, it won't happen again."

"I'm not concerned about that." He stared at me for a long time as I stood in silence, unsure about what he meant. He scratched the back of his neck, uncomfortably. "I, umm, wanted to know... how your mother is doing. If, if you don't mind me asking, of course."

I looked up at him with surprise. No. I did not just hear that. He clearly had another agenda. The wellbeing of my mother was something that would never cross his mind, surely. He didn't care about anyone but himself. Right?

Then I remembered what he said the other night. He got into a fight defending his own mother. It gave some reason, but not enough to explain why he was suddenly so interested. The camp was full of suffering mothers and grandmothers and he had no problem with putting them down.

I didn't answer his question. My mother was gone and I frankly didn't care what his reaction to that would be. Apparently, that spoke enough to him.

"I'm so sorry, Hana." My uninjured hand balled into a fist once more.

"I don't want your sympathy." I exclaimed, angrier than I should be.

"I understand that, but I wanted you to know that I am sorry. If you told me before that your mother was sick, I would have let you go."

"Why do you even care about what happens to her?" I found my anger shout as I flailed my arms, ready to cry. His face steeled.

"I don't. I just don't want you working inefficiently." He stated, quickly picking up his pen to get back to doing whatever he was. I tensed, fumed by his erratic behaviour.

"Would that be all?" I asked with as much respect I could muster, teeth clenched.

"No." He put his pen down again. "I understand that you're mourning. I'm annoyed that you are even here and that your grief is going to get in the way of the efficiency of this household. I insist you go back to the camps and get some rest before you return."

Stunned by his offer, my eyes widened. A day off. There was no such thing as a day off here. It was work, work, work. He was offering me a day to actually mourn my mother's passing. His hesitancy made me feel unsure whether he was giving me this gift for the "efficiency of this household" or not, but I was ecstatic at the news. But it was already too good to be true.

"I can't. No one is in the camps. They will be suspicious." I explained, disappointment lacing my tone. If they see me alone there, they would assume I was hiding away from my duties and shoot me before I even had the chance to explain.

"You're right." He agreed, looking thoughtful. "You can stay in here until nightfall and then you can be with your sister. I won't put you to any work so long as you don't tell anyone about our arrangement."

"Thank you." My voice was small but he had heard me and gave a small nod. He gestured to some chairs at the end of the room where I went to sit quietly.

I watched him closely as he worked for hours at his desk. Once, he got up to get himself a cup of coffee and then got straight back down to work again. He got out maps, documents, telegrams. I was glad he ignored me as I sat silently, dwelling on memories of my family.

Later on, he left the room once more. The room resembled his bedroom similarly, with dark furnishing contrasting by the white walls and the light floor. I stood up and started walking around the room, drained from all the sitting down.

I found my way to his desk, intrigued by all the items messily arranged. The globe in the corner had pins stuck in at different points with little notes attached, each with encrypted numbers on them. Several dossiers were littered around the table on some of the most powerful men in the world alongside high importance telegrams straight from Berlin. A map was spread out in the centre with little figurines representing the German army, French, British and Russian within various countries. In the corner, there lay a little note in cursive handwriting, 'January 1940', just a few months from now.

"See here," a voice chimed from behind me, making me jump. I did not even notice Herr Diedrich walk into the room with a bowls of ice cream in either hand, his back pressed against mine. He set it down on his desk and pointed to the black figures on Ukraine and Czechoslovakia on the map. "Anarchists. Thousands of anarchists planning to stage a rebellion to reclaim Poland and Czechoslovakia from us. What the Anarchists don't know is that their foremen are actually Soviet Officers who intend to seize the land for Stalin and hide from the non-aggression pact. Only, they don't know that we have intel from the inside so we are already tracking their every move, months in advance."

"An uprising? But then Stalin will have all of the eastern front! We wouldn't stand a chance!" The realisation came to me gradually. Though we were fresh in war, the global rage seemed consuming.

I knew he shouldn't be telling me this information at all, but there was an itch in me to know more.

"Wouldn't that make you happy, though? Aren't you a Communist?" He questioned, teasingly.

"I'm against the brutality of the Nazi regime. But if what you are saying is true then Stalin will eventually get Germany. I don't want that." As any German, I wanted war to be as away from home as possible. I didn't want to see Germany crippled again under another autocrat who didn't care for Germany at heart. "And for the love of god, I'm not a communist."

"You do like vanilla, yes?" He lifted up a bowl of Neapolitan ice cream to me and I was prepared to drown in how desirable it looked, regardless of the frosty September weather. It had been so long since I have had decent food to eat, never mind ice cream. I nodded, noticing his bowl consisted of just strawberry and chocolate. He frowned, disappointedly. "I figured you were weird. Only Communists enjoy vanilla ice cream, I'm telling you."

"Thank you." I smiled, accepting the bowl and not bothering to correct him again about my political standing. My focus turned back to the map. "So what are you going to do about the Anarchists?"

"See, this is a map of January 1940. Do you want to see the map of February 1940?" I watched eagerly as his hand swept away the black figurines from the map and onto the floor with a loud clattering noise. "Ta-dah!"

"You're going to kill them all?" Though I held a look of disbelief, I already knew the answer to my question.

"Look at you, Hana." He patted my head proudly. "You would make a good soldier if you were a man."

"But so many people will die. How can you just live with that?" He rolled his eyes, unfeelingly, taking a seat at his desk.

"We're not going to kill all of them. Just the forepeople. Our informant has given us twenty dossiers of the Soviet men in charge. If we can dismantle them, there won't be a problem and no one would have to know either side even broke the non-aggression pact. It will provide an illusion of mutual victory when, in fact, Germany will ultimately succeed. A silent war."

"I thought Anarchists don't even have leaders." I wasn't a very war orientated person. I steered away from violence as much as I could. But now it felt real and right in my face. Danger.

"This isn't a petty riot, Hana." He gave me a cold look. "This is war. You can't just fight it without conduction even if you have millions of followers. You just don't have to show the leaders to the world and keep up your facade, that's how Anarchists get away with it. After all, Anarchism is just failed mechanics."

Stuffing a spoon full of ice cream in my mouth, I tried to freeze out the images of death, knowing that this was for the greater good of Germany. People would die, but he was right. This is war. War cannot be fought without bloodshed, despite how much you want to preserve purity.

"Sit down." He offered and I sat opposite him at his desk. We ate our ice cream in silence for a while as I stared blankly at the map missing of the black figurines.

War.

My homeland was at war and I was in a labour camp, contemplating the fate of my country after losing another quarter of my family when I should have been at school, learning about things like childcare and eugenics.

"You know, my mother used to say that maps weren't made to document what we already know but to navigate the seas because they are the one thing we are too terrified to explore. She said that people think if we can put it down on paper, it's supposed to make it less intimidating for the people who can't take the fact that there is something bigger in the world than just us. That's why we try to map out the stars and the universe to even the microscopic cells of our body. Because we are scared."

"She sounds like an intelligent woman." I noted, hazed by the impactful words. She was right. Scared. We are nothing more than scared.

"What was your mother like?" He asked, sincerely, watching me closely over the rim of his ice cream bowl.

I thought for a small second that I could not answer. I thought if I tried to think about her too much, I would end up in an ocean of tears once more. However, I found that the words came naturally instead, as if they were sitting at the end of my tongue, waiting to be set free.

"Smart, like your mother. She would tell me things like that too. She was beautiful and loving and, more than anything, she was strong." I let out a small laugh, reminiscing on her unique character. "She would fight for what she believes in and she would suffer for what she loves. She was remarkable."

"She sounds like she would make a good soldier too. She sounds like you a lot." The corners of my lips rose into a smile, a common habit whenever someone compared me to my mother. It was flattering and incomparable to any other compliment, although I didn't know quite how to feel about him considering her able to be a good soldier.

A few more minutes passed in a well needed silence after all the noise of the past few days. Even with him sitting there, I did not feel uncomfortable. I knew, inside, that should have alarmed me, but I let it slide this once. I had lost my mother quicker than I could have ever imagined and a little company didn't feel that bad. When the clock tower bell rang from outside to mark nine pm, he looked somewhat dismayed.

"There should be some people in the camps now so I think you're safe to go. These documents are classified so don't tell anyone I told you about these."

Part of me was disappointed to leave. In the camps, people made alliances. Girls made friends and talked to each other comfortably. I only had Lola and my mother and now I was left with just Lola, who I was responsible of.

Having someone to talk to, despite how little it may be, felt alleviating. Even if it was just listing the characteristics of my mother, it felt calming to get it off my chest.

"Hana." He called, just as I was about to leave. His voice was shaky now, almost as if he was nervous. "Look, about the other day. I'm sorry. I shouldn't have slapped you. That was wrong of me."

There it was again. Warmth. He lit a small flame to flicker in me, growing every time he would expose the vulnerable side of him. It gave me hope.

"My mother taught me that forgiveness is the greatest weapon a person has. I would be letting her down if I didn't follow what she told me."

He was sober. He had forgotten that he apologised to me already. He meant it when he said sorry this time and that was what led me to forgive him.

But then again, he didn't apologise for what he did to me before, which was undeniably worse. I felt the little flame inside of me rapidly burn out.

I was lost in a maze of confusion. I assured myself he was a heartless monster. I knew that the fact I stayed with him two nights ago wasn't his fault. I knew the fact that he hit me the other day was incited by me and carried out by his ingrained patriotism. Harsh discipline. But in the end, it didn't change the fact that he raped me. He used my body like a rag doll catering to his every whim. That night, he was a heartless monster but tonight, he seemed genuine. He sounded like he actually cared.

"Your sporadic acts of kindness clouds my judgement." I let out with a sigh, making him chuckle.

"Goodnight, Amsel." He mused, smiling feverishly.

"Goodnight, Herr Diedrich."

•••

A/N

I've had a severe case of writers block for a while but hopefully you still enjoyed this chapter!

Also... Team Hans or Team Oskar? Hmm...

Like/Comment/Follow

Also, I think it's party time...

Chapter 6

- -

A gruelling month had passed after Mama had died, leaving me and Lola to fend for ourselves. It was difficult, to say the least. We all worked in different stations but it was the regular support and confirmation our mother provided that really kept us going. But that was lost now.

My interactions with Herr Diedrich improved, compared to our first few encounters. I found he was spending more time at home rather than outside, in his study or in his room, tactfully avoiding his father who no one really saw much of.

By improve, I meant he had resorted to ignoring me completely.

I didn't know why. I didn't recall doing anything wrong. Since the incident with the map and the ice cream, he greeted me with a coldness and hostility that was unbearably unlike him. Or maybe it was exactly like him.

It was becoming infuriating. In a day, he would speak to me the bare minimum, ordering me to get him a new pen or to clean up some juice he spilled and then he would completely overlook my presence when I was in the same room as him. Fair enough, that was supposed to be standard of our association, but it seemed too sudden and too rash for it to be meaningless, especially after how compassionate he was following my mother's demise.

Nonetheless, I didn't want his attention. I kept reminding myself he was a horrible person and then all the images of the monstrous things he had done came crashing back.

I did not dwell on it much because I was grateful for the additional food he would occasionally slip me for myself and Lola, relieving me a lot of stress about my sister's wellbeing, my primary concern. Lola didn't know how to take the news of mother's death. She just cried a little and then asked when she was going to wake up again the following day.

As for Matron, nothing changed with her. She thought I was as much of a nuisance as she did from the day she met me.

"Get the phone and try to sound polite, for once." She ordered, walking in the opposite direction of the blaring rings from the home telephone. Disregarding her comment, I head for the rotary dial telephone sitting on its small, circular table. "Diedrich household."

"I want to talk to Oskar." The person on the other side answered slowly, the vowels of his name big in her mouth. My lips curved up into a smile at the adorable little voice.

"May I ask who this is, please?" I replied, rallying the most cordial tone I could in my attempt to 'sound polite, for once'.

"Tell him it's his favourite. He'll know." A little giggle was heard on the receiving end, quickly muted by an older woman scolding the child in the background.

"Alright. One moment, please."

I groaned at the knowledge I would have to speak to him today, something I had learnt to dread since the moment he decided it was fit to cut off all the sympathy he expressed towards me before. Gulping down the lump in my throat, I knocked on his door and entered his room. He looked up and then back down to the book at hand with a scowl when he realised it was me.

"There's someone on the phone for you. She said to tell you that it's your favourite." His eyes beamed up with excitement as he leaped out of his bed and went downstairs, abruptly shoving past me on his way out.

"Elsa, what did I tell you about me not having a favourite?" He laughed, genuine happiness emanating from him as he spoke on the phone for four hours with three other people as well. I gathered it was his family; three sisters and his mother. I waited by his side, ready to serve him, if need be. When he was done, he glowered at me before walking away with another shove.

I kept my cool, knowing there was nothing I could do.

At around ten, when I was expecting to be let off to go back to the camps, Matron called me behind.

"And where do you think you're going?" She beckoned, grabbing my shoulder and pulling me back to the kitchens. "Oskar's friends are throwing him a party. You will be serving. It's a pretty difficult job to mess up, so don't."

"A party? For what?" I moaned, disappointed just when I thought I got off early.

"It's his birthday."

"Oh." I said, flatly. It completely surpassed my mind that he was born of natural human circumstances. "How old is he?"

"Nineteen, as of today."

"Oh."

The party did not start until midnight, but it was about one am when the house started filling up with masses of people (even though it was officially not his birthday anymore). Herr Diedrich did not involve himself much in conversation, though I did not depict him as very people shy. He shook hands, smiled and said 'thank you' when wished happy birthday and sat with a group of three talkative friends, but he was more engrossed in his glass of wine which he had me consistently refilling.

A light buzz permeated through the air, filled with the smoke of cigars and drunken laughter. The living room was dimly lit, darkness enclosing the drunken men taking off to different parts of the house with even more drunken girls, unquestioned. It made me sick to my stomach, but I clutched the bottle of wine tighter in my hand and pushed those thoughts out. Fresh talk of war murmured through the room as the guests sat in the home of an almighty Reichsführer, but all in all, the atmosphere was easygoing and fit for a King-To-Be's nineteenth birthday party.

I stood invisibly behind the sofa Herr Diedrich was slouched back on, surrounded by a group of close knit friends. I hadn't encountered any of his companions since he never invited them to his house but preferred meeting them elsewhere. When Herr Diedrich would finish the wine at hand, he lifted his glass and I would promptly refill it, and the same for his friends. He did not look particularly pleased with his blank expression as he was hunched back on the sofa, on his fourth glass.

"... which is why they parted ways." A blond said, finishing an inside joke. No one laughed. Herr Diedrich assumed a no-reaction policy. The other blond only smiled in response. The redhead looked incredibly confused.

"I don't get it." The redhead responded, scrunching his eyebrows together.

"Of course you don't get it, Daniel. Your mother told me your legs came out before your head did." The first blond replied, shaking his head in amusement.

"I don't get that either." The redhead, Daniel, frowned.

"It's okay, buddy. Just keep drinking." The second blond patted Daniel's back, taking another sip of his own drink, finishing the glass.

I went to his side and filled it up again, noticing the piercing glare Herr Diedrich was giving me. I cleared my throat softly, uncomfortable under his close watch. His attention was quickly diverted when two gorgeous girls leaned over his shoulders from behind the sofa, both simultaneously placing a kiss on his cheek. I looked away, uninterested in his female interactions.

"Oskar," one girl purred in his ear. "Some of the boys are playing poker outside. They're asking if you want to join."

"No," was his blunt response.

The girls exchanged a confused glance before walking away, looking slightly offended.

"What the hell was that, Diedrich?" The first blond raised an eyebrow.

"What, Joseph?" Herr Diedrich took a long sip of his wine.

"You refused two decent girls in one go. What's wrong with you?"

"Nothing." His eyes flickered to me for a brief second. "They seemed bland."

That was unforeseen, since I had witnessed Herr Diedrich bring many other girls into his room, all of similar physical appearance. Slender, doe eyes, beautiful skin. He was quite the womaniser, to say the least. Every morning after he brought a girl back, I would watch as they left his house alone, some in tears and some infuriated.

"At least you get to be picky." Daniel sulked. "The only girl that didn't walk away when I tried to talk to her was Sally from the grocers when I asked her where the eggs were."

"It's the hair, Dan." The other blond ruffled his striking red hair, spilling some alcohol on his lap in a state of drunkenness.

"It's the hair, Dan." The redhead mimicked, sighing and falling back on the sofa. "Oskar, please teach me your ways."

Then, when Herr Diedrich looked at me once again, I averted my eyes to the landscape painting on the wall.

He raped me. He raped me. He raped me.

He didn't have a 'way' but if you had to put a name on it, it would be force.

"Good evening, boys." A deep voice entered, causing the three guests to stand with a straight posture in spite of the evident influence of alcohol over them.

"Seig Heil!" They saluted Reichsführer Diedrich with their complete respect, eyes wide at his unprecedented appearance. Herr Diedrich remained sat on the sofa, drinking his wine.

"Why, Oskar, is there something wrong with your legs?" Reichsführer asked his son, sneeringly.

Herr Diedrich rolled his eyes with, thankfully, his back still faced to his father before standing up and chanting in a drunken slur, "Seig Heil, father! Seig Heil!"

Looking very displeased, Reichsführer pursed his lips. "You boys have a good night. I'm going upstairs now." He shot one more dirty look at Herr Diedrich, not offering any affectionate birthday wishes before exiting the room and going upstairs, receiving many glances of admiration on his way.

"Stop kissing my father's ass." Herr Diedrich looked equally irritated as he slumped back down on the sofa. He lifted his empty glass in the air and I went to refill it.

"You're joking, right?" Daniel raised his eyebrows. "You're so lucky to have a father like him. If I did, I would be kissing his ass, for sure."

"Shut up, Daniel."

Another half an hour passed of light conversation. Not many people bothered Herr Diedrich. The boys resumed simple conversation. I stood patiently by their side, trying my best not to eavesdrop on what they were talking about.

The blond man, who I still had not yet caught the name of, had once again downed his glass, being the fastest drinker of the four. Herr Diedrich was drinking a fair amount but slowly, as his usual habit. The blond looked at me and lifted his glass before turning his attention back to the playful conversation between Daniel and Jospeh as Herr Diedrich sat in silence.

The red liquid fell into the hollow glass swiftly. The bottle was lighter now than when it was first opened, making it easier to manoeuvre. When I finished pouring the glass, I intended to return to my position behind Herr Diedrich, but was stopped.

Before I could move, a cold hand travelled up my dress and wrapped tightly around my thigh, holding me in place.

I gasped. His hand moved up my leg, close to my sensitive zone. His thumb made small, circular motions on my upper thigh, sending shocks of dread through my skin that melted into my boiling blood.

I felt paralysed.

I bit my lip to stop it from quivering, knowing I did not have the authority to move out of his hold. The conversation between the three continued as his hand remained up my dress. I was certain that all three boys had noticed he was touching me since I didn't revert to my normal position and by the uncomfortable look on my face, but they did nothing.

I looked at Herr Diedrich with pleading eyes, knowing better. He had done the same to me. He had used me. He had dehumanised me. Why should his friend touching me now bother him?

"Stop that, Klaus. Can't we all just enjoy the drinks tonight?" Herr Diedrich leaned forward to pull Klaus' arm out of my dress. I let out a deep breath of relief, hurriedly moving back behind Herr Diedrich, shivering. The room had suddenly dropped miles in temperature as goosebumps formed on my skin.

"Okay, Diedrich. What's up your ass today?" Joseph queried.

"Nothing is up my ass." He defended himself, actively avoiding eye contact with me.

I should have been thankful for what he did. He stopped me from being used again. Again. Again, from the time he had used me himself.

"There's seriously something stuck up your ass." Daniel nodded in agreement. His face turned as red as his hair when Herr Diedrich gave him a scornful glare.

"Oh, I get it! She's your current one, isn't she?" Klaus raised his eyebrows, suggestively. I did my best to not look at him at all despite him being directly opposite me.

"No!" Herr Diedrich looked unamused. "She's from the camps. You shouldn't be touching her."

"She's a Jew?"

"No, but-"

"Then what's the problem? Unless she's already yours?" Joseph looked at him suspiciously again. I could feel a carnival of anxiety going off in my stomach.

"You know what, I'm tired. I'm going to bed." Herr Diedrich tried to stand but fell back with the force of alcohol, only to then successfully stand up again before promptly heading for the door.

"Come on, Oskar. It's your birthday. We were just kidding." That didn't seem to stop him as he set his glass down on a tray a waiter was walking by with and left the room.

Somewhere in me, I was frightened to see him leave, knowing that if he went, nobody would be here to stop anyone else from touching me the way his friend just did. I was trembling as it was, the bottle of wine shaking in my hands.

Like an answer to my prayers, he popped back into the room and called out, "Hana!"

Without missing a beat, I followed out with him, indulging in the sound of music and chatter fading away.

He stumbled up the stairs and pushed me back when I tried to help him. I bit my lip, defeated. When he finally got up the flight without any of my assistance, he went into his room and shut the door after I entered after him.

Herr Diedrich exhaled heavily, leaning against the door for support with his eyes firmly shut.

"Take your dress off." He ordered, anger leathering his tone. I froze. "Now, Hana!"

Not again. Please, not again.

Feeling his rage prick my skin, I didn't question him again. With shaking hands, I unbuttoned my dress and stepped out of it, tears stinging my eyes.

Fear transformed into perplexity when he walked over to his chest drawings to pull out a plain grey shirt which he flung at me.

"Put it on then!" Fire seeped through his voice as he threw his arms up hysterically. I did as he said in a rush of apprehension, pulling his shirt over my shoulders at his command.

My erratic breathing calmed, knowing he was not planning on touching me. I did my best to retain composure, remembering he owned me, leaving me no space to question his acrimony.

He approached me, either hand clutching onto my arm, pushing me backwards. I let out a small squeal when my legs hit his bed, causing me to fall back on it. His coordination was poor and mishandled and I had no idea how to react to it.

"Go to sleep, then! You look tired!" His voice was rough and his eyes were locked on me as I fumbled with his duvet, pulling it over my shaking body.

He was unleashing his long held wrath and I fell victim to the impact. I was crawled up into a ball in his duvet, failing to anticipate his next moves, any of which could be fatal.

I felt the mattress depreciate as he gently sat down on the side of the bed, head in his hands.

"Herr Diedrich, is everything okay?" I asked, carefully. I sat up, a nervous tugging in my chest as the sound of his heavy breathing quietened.

"No, Hana. Everything is not okay!" He twisted round and lowered his head until his face was hovering above mine. The smell of alcohol was evident on him. "He shouldn't have touched you. It got me so mad. More mad than it should have. I shouldn't have touched you. I should never have touched you. God, I'm such an idiot!"

Silence.

That's all I could respond with. Silence.

It didn't make sense. There was no way he could feel remorse. He wasn't a remorseful person. He was angry and drunk and confused. I refused to believe it.

"Is that why you have been ignoring me?" I asked, nonetheless.

"You don't get it do you." His jaw clenched. "Every time I look at you, there are things I want to do to you. The amount of times I've fantasised about you, Hana. The amount of times I've pictured you in my bed, mine to hold." His warm breath tickled my ear. "God, the things I would do to you... if you were mine." He paused, moving back. "But you're not. So I won't. I regret hurting you so much and there's nothing I can do to take it back and every time I look at you I want to say sorry, but I'm too much of a coward."

I was sitting docile in a whirlwind. I knew he had an affectionate side. I saw it when he spoke to his mother and his sisters. I knew he had a forgiving side. I saw it when he apologised for hitting me. But I also knew he had a dangerous side and I saw it every second of everyday when he had a gun by his side and a Swastika on his arm but it seemed to dissipate when he was like this.

You're fooling yourself, Hana.

"Just go to sleep." His voice was breaking. "Forget I said anything."

I didn't get any sleep that night.

All I could do was replay his words in my head.

There are things I want to do to you, Hana.

I lied down on my side, gripping the pillow tightly to myself.

The amount of times I've pictured you in my bed, mine to hold.

Once more, the graphic flashes of the first night we met came soaring back in a havoc.

I should never have touched you.

And then there was the great ordeal of his unspoken apology that felt real, but left me more torn than ever.

... but I'm too much of a coward.

Chapter 7

- -

A long night pursued after Herr Diedrich's fiery outburst. I expected him to pass out after all the glasses he had downed, but much to my dismay, he was still awake an hour after he told me how regretful he felt.

I did not know whether to believe it or not. He was drunk and behaving irrationally as it was. He had sisters. He knew the kind of pain and trauma he could inflict from even before he did it. And, after all, I was just a spec of dust drowning in a sea of all the girls he had been affiliated with. Only, I was dropped in the middle, directionless.

I questioned whether his words were his untainted thoughts or simply false. It would explain why he had been giving me the silent treatment for over a month. It would explain why he would not look at me unless it was absolutely necessary or to shoot me a scowl.

The troubles of that matter fell to the back of mind, encaged between the dreadful memories of that night and the imminent palpitations provoked by my long held fear.

I was locked in a frame of tremor.

My face was sodden with sweat and my hands were trembling by my side. I could feel the oxygen rushing in and out of my lungs as my chest rose and fell in rapid motion, misaligned with my irregular heartbeats screaming in my ear as blood flushed through my body.

"Hana," came a gentle voice next to me. "What's wrong?"

My head snapped to the direction of the sound to match a face with the voice. The incoming moonlight casted a silhouette over his head but was too faint to keep the room alight.

When he places a hand on my shoulder, I realised that I was crying.

Streams of tears flooded down my face. The ache in my eyes caused a heaviness to my head that pulsed with every heavy breath. I clutched the duvets tighter to myself, discomfort pervading every corner of my body.

"I'm scared." I croaked out, too vulnerable to cover it up. Eyes set on the wall with my mind somewhere else, I couldn't catch his reaction.

"Of me?" His voice was strained, as if hurt. I twisted my head to face him again, the deafening silence torn apart by my futile cries.

"No." The word was almost a whisper, every other sound being caught in the cobwebs of my throat. "Of the dark."

After a moment of silence, an arm leaned over my body to turn on the bedside lamp, instantly flooding the room with a golden glow.

A soft sigh escaped his lips. "Why didn't you tell me before?"

My lungs lost the capacity to utter any more words. I lied down silently, leaving his question unanswered as I tried to calm down my fluctuating heart rate.

Light.

There was light again. The room was lit with the soothing waves of a single light bulb, emanating its comfort, which I clutched onto with dear life. The off-white walls adorned the dancing shadows as the mirror echoed the light across the room.

I felt safe again.

Or at least, safer.

My sleep broke in the early hours of a Sunday morning as the blazing sunlight trickled in through the gap in the curtains, blinding me.

I blinked tightly, finding it impossible to escape the imperious flood of light overtaking everything in my vision. Reluctantly, I force myself out of the invitingly warm bed and push myself towards the window. Fresh morning dew had settled on the window pane as the sun welcomed in the new day.

Light.

It felt so comforting.

"Good morning." I jumped at the sudden sound, accidentally hitting my wrist hard on the windowsill. Cradling my arm, I turn around to see the familiar voice. "Did I scare you?"

I shook my head way too fast, watching as he grinned amusedly whilst pressing his face against his pillow.

It dawned on me that I wasn't back at my home in Berlin.

By the bed he was lying on sat a little lamp, still turned out but its light was drowned by the incoming sunlight. Then, I looked down and noticed the unfamiliar grey shirt I was wearing that fell to my mid-thigh, exposing the rest of my legs. Looking up once more, a boy was half awake on one side of the bed I had just awoken from, with his arms splayed across the pillow.

I wasn't in Berlin at all.

At this rate, anyone would think that I was the one drinking last night and not him.

"Shouldn't you be downstairs?" His voice was still rough with sleep as closed his eyes tightly, presumably because of the ache in his head from all that he had drank last night.

For a moment, I wondered what he meant by 'be downstairs', until it hit me. I swivelled around and groaned with annoyance as I viewed the daylight again, which meant it was past sunrise hour and much too late to be five am.

Matron was going to have my head on a platter!

I head for the door in lightning speed, fumbling with the doorknob in a flurry of haste, stopped by an awkward cough and a mumbled "Hana."

"Yes?" I tapped my foot, impatient to leave. His head gestured towards an item of clothing at the foot of the bed.

My dress. Of course. I was still in his shirt.

I coughed, awkwardly. He responded by placing his hand over his eyes, though I was sure he was peeking. Nonetheless, I didn't have time to waste so I hurried to the corner of the room and changed into my outfit before running out of the door.

I briskly did up the last buttons of my dress, closing the door behind me. It was in that precise moment (as coincidental as it may sound), I bumped into Hans, the top button of my dress still left to go.

"Hana?" He looked as if he had seen a ghost, his gaze switching between my undone button and Herr Diedrich's door behind me. He started walking away with the laundry basket sitting in his hands.

"Hans, wait!" I called out, running down the stairs after him. "Ah!" I cried, as he tugged my arm and pulled me into the cupboard under the smaller staircase of the house. He closed the door and turned the overhead lamp on and exhibited a great expression of worry.

"Hana, are you okay? Did he... Did he... Again...?" He stuttered with his words, careful where to tread despite being full of concern.

"No, Hans. It's nothing like that." I assured. "That was only the once."

"Then why did you spend the night in his room? And why were you doing up your dress?" He looked befuddled, eyes searching for some explanation as they scoured mine. "Did you sleep with him?"

"No." I paused. "Yes, kind of, but it's not–"

"Hana, he used you." He enclosed his hand around mine, instantly making me feel guilty.

I had been trying to put off thinking about it for so long, I wasn't sure if it even happened. But it did, didn't it? Herr Diedrich apologised. He felt remorseful. That's all I could have asked from him.

"That was different, Hans. He was a different person."

Was I trying to convince him, or myself?

"People don't change like that." He squeezed my hand, looking at me straight in the eyes. "We're animals of habit, and he'll just go back to his. You're setting yourself up to be hurt again. People like him will never know the meaning of reform."

"You don't know him –"

"And you do?" He stated, sharply. "He's a Nazi, Hana. He is the reason you are here and not in your home in the free side of Germany. Stop being so naive!"

I wasn't being naive. I knew Herr Diedrich. I knew how far he would go. It wasn't unchartered territories I was stepping on anymore. I knew exactly what I was doing!

"Hans will you please just mind your own business?" I could feel the annoyance bleeding out of me as I pulled my hand away from his. "Nothing I do with him should concern you."

And it wasn't like I offered to sleep next to him last night. He forced me to. He ordered me to go to sleep there and, if anyone, Hans should have understood what following orders meant around here.

"I'm not sorry I care about you." He looked down, taking a small step back. I gulped, not expecting to have heard that. Maybe I shouldn't have snapped at him like that.

"Hans, this isn't a place where people care about people." I hushed my tone, realising he didn't mean any harm. "Even if you do, bad things still happen. No one is protected because of something as trivial as concern."

He scoffed and let out a humourless laugh. "Right, but you are protected because you're sleeping with him? Is that what it is?"

My insides flipped.

I was speechless, unsure if I really heard what I just did.

"That was just low, Hans." I grabbed the door handle violently, boiling rage restless inside of me. "And for the record, I'm not sleeping with him. Even if I was, it would be none of your business."

I stomped out of the closet, steam spewing out of my ears, with Hans following behind me. If that wasn't bad enough, my argument with Hans followed with me bumping into Herr Diedrich, who was coming down for breakfast, whilst exiting the small storage cupboard beneath the staircase, with Hans.

"G-good morning, H-Herr Diedrich." Hans stammered, bowing his head down.

Herr Diedrich exchanged an incredibly confused glance between me and Hans, and then me and Hans again, and then me and the door behind me and then Hans, once more. He walked away without saying another word, whistling to himself casually as if he had seen nothing at all.

I gave Hans another glare before heading to the kitchen, unprepared for whatever lecture Matron was going to throw at me today.

"Are we not going to talk about what happened earlier?" I leaped, suddenly disrupted as I was scrubbing the wooden floors of Herr Diedrich's bedroom.

What was it with everyone today and sneaking up on me?

He was home early again. It was only six in the evening, when he would usually be out and I would clean his room without any distractions.

"With Hans? Oh, it was nothing." I insisted, turning back to the sponge in my hand.

"No, not that. I couldn't care less about him." He took his jacket off and sat on his chaise, directly in front of me. I focussed on the lathering bubbles forming on the floor. "About last night. When I apologised and you had a dramatic breakdown because you were scared of the –"

"That wasn't a nightmare?" I bit my lip, trying to recall what happened as much as I could.

"No." He leaned forward, lifting my chin with his hand. "You started crying for your mother and you were tugging on the duvet like a madwoman. What happened?"

"I... I don't know." I whispered.

The last time I had an episode like that was when I was thirteen.

Mama was staying with grandmother in Hamburg, who had fallen fatally ill. Lola and I were alone in the house, stranded with my father whilst a power cut had darkened my entire neighbourhood. It was late at night, nearing three am and he was drinking more than he should have, unchecked by my absent mother. He was shouting in a drunken range, breaking vases and photo frames and pointlessly screaming at my sleeping neighbours.

I couldn't sleep, begging to hold Mama, knowing there was nothing I could do but sit through the dreadful night, hearing my father shout his life into ruins.

Maybe I relapsed because it was all too familiar. Drunken man. Missing mother. Absolute helplessness.

I hated it here, in the camps. I wanted to go home.

"Why are you here, Hana?" I was snapped back into reality at Herr Diedrich's question.

"Oh... well, the floor wasn't polished enough and Matron –"

He rolled his eyes. "I know that, you fool. I meant, why are you in the camps? If you are not a Communist, then what did you do to deserve that red triangle?"

I dropped the sponge back into the bucket, leaning back to sit on my ankles. I couldn't evade his question as much as I wanted to. He could find out easily by asking anyone in the camps, but he decided to ask me directly instead. A part of me was intimidated. A part of me was glad I could explain for myself.

"Nothing." I swallowed down my fear when I saw him raise his eyebrow. "My neighbour was a Democrat. My mother was a nurse. He was shot by the Gestapo in the leg and my mother helped him recover on our living room sofa. Apparently that was sufficient to earn her a bullet in the head and to send our family here."

I left out the part where my father claimed it was all him and that he had forced my mother into nursing the innocent man, despite not knowing of her acts at all, amidst his drunken fiasco. In the end, he had taken a bullet to his head to protect his wife, who he had loved for eighteen years and had also neglected for the last four, in a final act of artificial love.

"Oh, wow."

Neither of us said anything in the moments following. I watched the white lace of the bubbles on the floor swirl around like the world was a peaceful place and like hell did not belong on earth.

"I might have been drunk last night, but I meant what I said. If I remember correctly, I apologised for... for doing what I did to you. I am sorry. I mean it." He was twisting his hands together on his lap, eyes easily caught by anything in the room, but me.

Forgiveness.

Forgiveness was a chore for some and a gift for others. It was held in the hands of angels and prided by the thorns of the devil. Forgiveness was the glue that would hold the world together and the cement that would keep stories apart at the same time.

"Okay."

It didn't feel like a chore or a gift at this point. It didn't even feel like a duty. It felt empty. It felt pointless. But it felt necessary and I did not know if I had the strength to offer it wholeheartedly yet.

Running a hand through his hair, he straightened his back and stood up. Gesturing to the half-washed floor, he said, "You can go now. Just tell someone to finish it up. You don't have to stay."

He turned his back to me and started fiddling with the vinyls in his shelf, seeming more preoccupied with other thoughts. Remembering I had not seen Lola last night, I was accepting of his offer, aware of how worried she would be.

"Thank you, Herr Diedrich." I peeled my gloves off my hand and headed out.

"Wait, Hana." He called, taking a vinyl out of its sleeve to put into the phonograph. "You can call me Oskar."

I nodded as I slipped out of the door, wondering if the shreds of me that had survived these past two months still held the power to forgive such merciless acts.

•••

Chapter 8

"Wash the plates again!"

"Fix your uniform!"

"Clean the portico!"

Matron's string of commands echoed across the basement, setting off an assembly of servants and on-roll prisoners to ready the house for the arrival of a very important guest.

You would think that by the 25th of December, someone as poorly clothed as me would be trapped in a cube of ice by now. In fact, it was quite the opposite.

I was sweating, running around in the kitchens like a madwoman who had just lost seventeen of her nineteen kittens. The kitchens were hot; steam from the ovens and the lack of ventilation creating a large boiling pot of frantic women and half empty sacks of fresh potatoes.

"Amsel, upstairs." I exhaled with happiness when Matron dismissed me from the kitchen to go up to Herr Di– Oskar's room. Two months later and I was still getting that wrong.

I took my apron off and ran upstairs, desperate to get out of that underground Amazonian climate. I was panting with great relief when I was hit with the fresh, Christmassy air of ground level.

When I entered Oskar's room, he was fresh out of a shower, shirtless, whilst drying his hair with a towel.

I couldn't help but keep my eyes off how unbelievably well built he was. For a person whose daily timetable consisted of drinking, sleeping and periodically killing, he was incredibly toned and muscular. His arms, his abdominal muscles, his chest. Everything about him seemed moulded by the hands of perfection itself.

He may not be a particularly good person, but he was definitely very handsome. The kind of guy girls fell for at first glance.

"Stop staring. You're making me feel self conscious."

"I wasn't staring." I claimed, sure that my cheeks were crimson. He smirked, whilst slipping on a formal shirt before throwing me a set of cufflinks. I walked over and put them on for him as he did up his buttons. "They're little Christmas trees!"

"My grandfather gave it to me." A small smile lit up on his face. The sound of a car approaching the front of the house filled the room. "See you later, then. Merry Christmas, Hana."

"Merry Christmas." I replied as he left the room. I went forth and tidied up after him, picking up the wet towel on his chair and then fixing his bed.

The last two months went by quite nicely. Oskar and I would talk about normal things, like the weather or how grumpy Matron looked that day on a scale of one to thirteen. He would usually let me go early so I could spend time talking with Lola and making sure she wasn't afraid when falling asleep in the stench of the cabins. It never got easier, dealing with mother's death, but I learnt how bury the pain deep inside so it wouldn't hurt as much and so I could still be there to coddle Lola.

With the slightest bit of curiosity, I leaned over the window frame to view the commotion outside.

One incredibly well dressed woman and her three girls stepped out of the car, the smallest of whom ran up to Oskar to enclose him in a tight hug. The second youngest followed suit but the oldest child just patted his shoulder. They were the three girls from the picture; his sisters!

The two oldest girls also went to greet Reichsführer but the smallest stayed in Oskar's arms as his supposed mother came to kiss his cheek. He was smiling like a child who had just been given a bag of sweets, surrounded by his family.

His mother was the definition of beautiful. Locks of her golden hair cascaded down the side of her face, falling effortlessly by her shoulders. Imperfection was nonexistent on her face, which shone with brightness whenever she smiled. She definitely did not look like a woman who have given birth to four children.

His mother and father exchanged a rather uncomfortable looking greeting before the six of them headed inside, trailed behind by Matron and her help.

It took me longer than usual to tidy up Oskar's room because of the slight distraction, but as soon I was done I went straight downstairs to help set up the table.

The dining room was empty except for the large and lavish dessert trays sitting by the side. Yule log, trifle, a pyramid of truffles, mince pies, you name it. It made my mouth water. We were lucky to have Mama's homemade chocolate cake during Christmas back at home, never mind a feast fit for royalty!

As I was about to grab the silverware to set the table, an arm slipped around my waist, pulling me away.

"Oskar!" I squealed as he suddenly pulled me closer until my midriff was pressed against his.

"Christmas desserts are always my favourite." He picked up a truffle covered in shavings of hazelnut and held it up to my mouth. I quickly pulled away, realising the compromising position we were standing in.

"What if someone sees?" I looked to the doorway, relieved when I was assured no one had passed by.

"No one is going to see, Hana." He sounded certain. "My family is busy upstairs and the help are busy downstairs. And even if they do see anything, what are they going to do about it? Tell me?"

The whole act caught me by surprise. The last time I was pressed up against him like that was... was a very long time ago. I didn't know why he had a sudden rush of affection. Maybe it was safest to steer clear of it all.

"Fine." With a pleased look, he tightened his grip around me again as I took a bite of the tempting truffle from his hand. It melted into a sea of smoothness in my mouth, a taste I had been craving for months.

By dinnertime, I had gathered some information. The eldest daughter who was soon to be fourteen, Adalina, had a very deep rooted dislike for her older brother. They shared the exact same scowl. The middle daughter, Carolina, was extremely shy and introverted, mumbling when necessary or staying to herself completely. The youngest child, whose voice I recognised, was Elsa, Oskar's six year old sister. She was the only one with blond hair and was extremely attached to her brother, latching onto him wherever he went.

His mother, who went by the name of Emma Diedrich, was six years divorced of the Reichsführer but still, strangely, attained his name. The tension between the two was very evident during their Christmas dinner, which everyone on the table and on the serving team (including myself) seemed to notice.

"Damien, will you pass me the salt, please." Frau Diedrich asked politely, from the opposite end of the table. Reichsführer muttered something under his breath before passing the salt shaker to Carolina to pass it to Frau Diedrich.

That was the only conversation they had the entire night.

I also realised that this was the first Christmas I was spending without my family. It wasn't that we did very much, but it was the only occasion in the year where we would force ourselves to get together and eat dinner around a table as a family. Now, I didn't even have the freedom to decorate a tree or listen to carollers passing by on my street. It made me feel lonely. I had lost my father and my mother and now Christmas too.

"Hana, some wine." Snapping out of my trance, I went to fill up Oskar's glass. That earned a questionable look from his mother, though I wasn't quite sure what about.

"Oskar, you are an adult now. I shouldn't still have to tell you to finish your vegetables." Displeased, she leered at his almost empty plate, only the peas remaining.

"Sorry, mother." Oskar's face started turning as green as the peas as he abided by his mother, battling on a forkful at a time. I could see how revolted he was, but nonetheless, he did not leave a pea remaining.

"Mama, look! I finished my vegetables!" Little Elsa beamed, pointing to her empty plate. Oskar patted her head, but she only received a grimace from her father. Her face dropped when she realised. The poor girl slumped back in her chair, arms down by her side.

"Ignore him, El. He's just jealous." I overheard Oskar whisper into her ear. The corners of my lips rose up at his affection for his youngest sibling.

It reminded me about what I first thought when I learnt about her.

I remembered what Matron said about him being a family person and it made me wonder what he would do if someone did what he did to me to his sister.

"Hana, is it?" Stopped on my way to Oskar's room, I turned to face Frau Diedrich and offered a small curtsy. I was curious as to how she knew my name.

"Yes, ma'am." I answered, nervously.

"Come in." She sounded cool and eloquent as she sat by the dressing table, taking off the pearls around her neck. I shut the door behind me, waiting patiently for whatever she needed me for. "Are you from the camps?"

"Y-yes, ma'am."

"And Oskar doesn't have you wear your star?" Her eyes twinkled with suspicion.

"I'm not a Jew." I corrected. "Herr Diedrich doesn't have me wear my triangle because he says he does not want to see it everyday."

"Hmm. Of course."

"Is there anything I can help you with?" I asked, bravely, aware of her watchful eye on me through the mirror. She slowly put her necklace into a satin-lined box, closing it shut with ease. She twisted around on the chair, making eye contact with me. Then, she looked down.

"Oskar..." I froze. "I raised him a good kid. I need you to tell me that his father has not ruined that for him."

I could feel something stuck in my throat. Oskar. A good person? I honestly did not know anymore.

Three months ago, I was sure he was evil. Sure. And now I did not even know the question I was being asked.

"I don't think I am the suitable person to answer that for you, I'm afraid." I answered with thought, trying to sound convincing.

"I do not think that is true." She gave me a knowing look. "It's not everyday that Oskar knows the name of a girl he is sleeping with."

What was it with everyone and assuming I'm sleeping with him!

"Oh... oh... I'm not... No!" A ghastly look took over my face. He had slept with me once, if you would even call it that.

"If you insist, a pretty girl like you." She walked up to me and held my hands in hers. "But I still want you to answer my question. Honestly, as well."

"Well," I paused for a moment. "He cares about his family and his country, which makes him a better person than you think."

Whether I meant what I said or not, seeing the invaluable relief and happiness on a mother's face was worth it.

"Thank you, Hana." She exhaled deeply, squeezing my hands. "Hana, you seem like a sweet girl. If Damien catches the slightest sniff of whatever is between you and my son, he will not hesitate to hurt you."

I could feel the chill of her words shake my spine. He was a dangerous man. I knew that. From the work he did in the camps to the gruesome rumours that circulated, he was a man of violence and bloodshed and I was walking around in his home on first name basis with his only son.

When her hands let go of mine, I left the room with her words still echoing in my head.

He won't hesitate to hurt you. He won't hesitate to hurt you. He won't hesita–

"Will you help me get ready for bed, please?" I looked down to the little girl responsible for the tugging on my dress.

"Of course, Miss Elsa." With a huge grin, she put her hand into mine and pulled me into Oskar's bedroom. "Are you sleeping in here?"

She nodded. "There aren't enough guest rooms so I always have to share with Mama or Oskar." I was certain that there were plenty guest rooms to fill a nation, or one small girl, at least.

She lifted her hands over head as I helped to take her dress off before putting on her silk nightgown. She reminded me a lot of Lola, only a wealthier version. They both had the same spark and energy and it twisted my heart knowing my sister's spark and energy was locked up in a death box.

"You're so pretty." She giggled whilst hoisting herself onto Oskar's chair in front of the dressing table so I could brush her hair.

"You think so? I think that you are prettier." She snickered childishly again.

"I'm Oskar's favourite girl." She stated out of the blue, nodding her head, assertively. Just as I was about to respond, Oskar entered the room, like on cue.

"Elsa." He warned. "You know I don't have a favourite."

"Yeah, sure." She ran into his bed, making herself snug and comfortable. "So when are you two getting married?"

I choked on the air.

Suddenly, the room felt excruciatingly suffocating.

"Excuse me?" Oskar cocked an eyebrow.

"Mama says if you don't get married soon you will get too wrinkly for any girl to want." Elsa explains, nonchalantly.

"Hey, I'm only nineteen! I have plenty of time to find the perfect woman." His eyes flickered to me for a split second. I quickly looked away.

Did all the air in the room suddenly decide to disappear?

"Yeah, well, she's already looking for a wife." Elsa played with her hair, lost in thought. "So far she has Luci from the Müller family who lives down the road and Donna from the department store."

"I'm not getting married anytime soon, Elsa. Sorry to burst your bubble." He looked equally uncomfortable, as well. At least I knew I was not alone.

"No, but you have to!" She whined, getting right into Oskar's face. "I have to be your maid of honour!"

"Elsa, I don't have a maid of honour." He stated, fed up. "Only the bride does."

She gasped, a look of horror storming through her eyes.

"No, that's no fair! Then what's my special role at your wedding?" She grumbled, burying her face in the pillow. Oskar sat down at the edge of the bed, scooping her onto his lap.

"Making my wife jealous by your charm and beauty and my undying love for you." The frown on her quickly wiped away.

"Hear that, Hana? His undying love for me!"

I would be lying if I said I wasn't slightly heartbroken that I wouldn't ever get married. I heard stories about people escaping their camps, but I knew I did not have the courage for that.

As a child, I always looked forward to getting married to a wonderful man. I looked forward to being greeted every day by the perfect husband and having children of my own. I looked forward to my father walking me down the aisle, but I lost hope of that dream a long time ago.

"Yes, Miss Elsa, I do."

She redirected her gaze to her brother. "You will still be the maid of honour at my wedding, right?"

"I'm afraid that's a girls job. I put my money on you choosing Carolina over Ada."

"That's not fair!" She crossed her arms over her chest, angrily. "What special job will you have at my wedding, then?"

"I'll walk you down the aisle, of course!"

"But mama said that's what my dad is supposed to do." She rested her head on Oskar's arm with disappointment.

I realised the rough relationship she had with her father at the dinner table and I empathised with her. Reichsführer definitely did not seem like he was very interested in his family. I had lost my father too, even though he was sitting right in front of me. Maybe it would have been easier if he wasn't there at all.

"Elsa, if I'm going to give you away to another man, I am going to be the one to do it and not any other lame guy. Same goes for your sisters." She sat up ecstatically, happiness filling her eyes. A candle lit in my heart at his gracious offer, instantly making me wish I had an older sibling like him when I was young, too.

Elsa wrapped her arms around his neck as I stood at the end of the room, watching their moment of tenderness.

When Adalina strolled into the room, both Elsa and Oskar looked disappointed, only Elsa was not as discreet. She looked to Oskar. "Here comes your least favourite."

"Elsa, I love Ada as much as I love you. We have been over this many times."

"There's a spider in my room so I am sleeping in here tonight." The girl made herself comfortable in Oskar's bed. "Get out, then."

With that, the three of us left the room; Oskar with his sister in his hands and me going off to see mine.

•••

Chapter 9

The next morning, Oskar decided to take the girls to Berlin and, for some reason, he wanted me to go with them. Only, Matron was not as keen on the idea.

"What if she runs?" She snarled. "I wouldn't put it past her."

"She won't. Her sister is still here." Oskar confirmed. "Someone has to carry our bags."

"So take another one. That one there is dangerous." I gasped.

Me? Dangerous? Dear god, I once cried after accidentally killing a ladybird!

A disgruntled Adalina stuck her head out of the car window. "If you don't hurry up, I am going to be as old and wrinkly as Oskar by the time we leave."

With that, Oskar entered the car, pulling me in with him. A sheet of snow blanketed the hood of the car, standing out against the black. The chilly air bit at my skin, causing me to shiver. Whilst everyone was cocooned in their coats and hats, I simply had my dress to offer me warmth as well as the coziness of the car with Oskar by my side.

When we reached Berlin, an uneasy feeling settled in my stomach as I peered out of the window.

My home.

It felt like it was hanging just beyond my fingertips, too far to reach but I could feel it lingering around my touch. I wanted to grasp it and cling onto the feeling of home, but it was lost from me and even if I tried to repossess it, the act would leave me for nothing but dead.

A river of Aryan children, parents and soldiers formed the bustling crowds of the Berlin streets. The area was formed of poised and affluent looking Berliners, the kind you would never see where I grew up. Luxury stores were lined up on either side of the street, increasing in exclusiveness as we progressed through. Newspaper stalls were propped equal increments apart, each headlining the latest progresses in war and each swarmed by their curious readers, eager to get their daily dosage of dinnertime conversation worthy news.

"Stop here." Oskar told the driver, who parked in front of a grand, palatial boutique.

"We're here! We're here! We're here!" Elsa sang, springing out of the door before the driver could have opened it for her. "Come on, then! Let's go inside!"

Ada and Carolina followed her and then Oskar, with me behind him. I stood in awe of the boutique; a glowing gem amidst a sea of other jewels. The mirrors inside glistened with the light reflected off from the outside snow. Dresses hung by either wall and two rows down the centre with cushioned seating elegantly placed around. An elderly woman crouched in a corner looked very preoccupied with her sewing machine and the unkempt bundles of fabric swamping her.

The girls went around selecting fabrics and shoes and matching jewellery for almost an hour. Oskar sat uncomfortably on a sofa as one of the sales clerks kept trying to force a conversation with him, in a creepily flirtatious tone. I helped the girls with zips, buttons, corsets and fittings, silently admiring the beauty and the breadth of their options that Lola and I never had.

"I will be back in a bit." Oskar informed, prying the eager salesgirl's hand off his shoulder. "Carolina, you're in charge."

"Why is she in charge?" Adalina looked horrified. "I'm the oldest!"

"No, I am. I make the rules." He asserted. "Carolina, are you okay with that?"

She nodded.

"Come on." He gestured towards me. I raised an eyebrow, sure that I was better here with the girls but followed him out of the store anyways.

"Where are we going?" I asked as we descended down the steps of the store.

"I need to get something."

Oskar headed westwards with long strides, making it difficult for me to keep up. His highly esteemed uniform received a few curious glances but he paid no attention to them. Where people parted on the pavements to make room for the reputable soldier passing by, I was trying to squeeze between the gaps and fight my way through.

After a while, he pulled me into a narrow alleyway, the opening enclosed between a barbers and a delicatessen.

The poignant stench of misery and decay instantly hit my face, very similar to the smell of the camps. The uneven, cobbled roads made my feet ache as I trudged along behind Oskar, doing my best not to trip.

Darkness overshadowed the thin pathway, leaving it to swim in the darkest charcoal. A single slit of light cut through the floor, that had managed to slither through the small partition between the almost touching roofs of the opposite buildings. Even the snow did not make it to the ground.

I started to feel apprehensive with the lack of light and the limited space to move. My breathing became more rapid as horrible thoughts pervaded my head. However, they soon washed away when a warm hand enclose over mine, pulling me on.

"There is nothing to be scared of. I'm here, don't worry." Oskar reassured, squeezing my hand lightly. My heart rate calmed down as I let his hand guide me to our destination.

He stopped in front of a door that would otherwise have been missed if not for memory, bearing an 'Open' sign that covered the window. The door opened with a large creaky sound, setting off an overhead bell. I walked in behind him, taking in the sight. It was unmistakable, even under the limited light.

Guns.

Lots and lots and lots of guns.

All types of guns. Big ones, small ones. All powerful guns. I did not know much about guns, but there were a lot.

"It's Diedrich. Get out here, Carl." He banged his fist on the empty desk twice, causing a stout, moustached man to grumpily enter from the back door.

"Herr Diedrich." The man bowed his head before turning to me. "Who's the girl?"

"Not your concern. Did you get what I requested?"

The shabby man let out a low, incomprehensible noise from the back of his throat. He turned to the door behind him to unlock it but stopped Oskar when he tried to enter.

"Your gun." He extended an awaiting hand out to his customer. Personally, I thought it was rather a ridiculous request considering there were plenty of guns out here anyways, but I did not go so far as to voice my opinions.

"What for?" Oskar resisted.

"Precautions. You know the protocol."

He pulled out the aforementioned item held at his waist and slid it across the counter towards Carl. His icy glare remained targeted at the man in the moustache when he followed him into the back room with me trailing behind them.

We walked passed the counter and entered the back of the store. It was darker than the front and at first, there was only blackness to view. However, when the man turned the light on, I was astonished by what I was met with.

Vinyls.

Lots and lots and lots of vinyls.

All types of vinyls. Pop, Jazz, American music. I knew a lot about vinyls, including the fact that none of these were spared under the Nazi censorship.

I was speechless. I was expecting bombs or other violent means of destruction. Not vinyls.

The shopkeeper crouched to the floor and rolled up part of his frayed carpet to reveal a hidden door. Meanwhile, Oskar was scouring through the range of music along the shelves. The fat man lifted the wooden door and leaned his hand into the crawlspace to come back with a knotted bag, covered in a thin layer of dust.

"They're all there." He claimed, handing the bag to Oskar. Oskar grabbed it from him and set it on a nearby table. I stayed quiet as he opened the bag and studied each sleeve and each disc with his utmost focus until he had consolidated that they were all real and up to his standards.

"Decent." He tied up the bag and handed it to me. I almost lose my balance at its weight with my feeble strength, but manage to keep my stand.

He pulls out an unbelievably large wad of cash and sets it on the table, but does not get the chance to move away. The man had grasped his arm, stopping him from leaving.

"Double."

"What? Why?" Infuriated, Oskar tugged his arm out of Carl's hold, who was looking at me with narrow eyes.

"Extra liability." He purses his lips with his eyes landing on me. Uncomfortable, I fumble with the plastic of the bag, looking to Oskar.

With evident resentment, he pulls out even more cash from his pocket and doubles the amount already on the table. I gape at the mountain of money, disbelieving that that much was even obtainable by a single person.

When the shopkeeper looked satisfied, he handed Oskar his gun and lead us out. Oskar once again held my empty hand and led me out of the store.

He walked down the alleyway slower than before. Much slower. I did not mind so much as I would have, since I knew if anything bad were to happen, he was here. Maybe him holding my hand played a part in that too.

A comfortable silence eased into the air. The alleyway stretched out quite a bit, giving me more time to revel in the warmth of his hand and hide from the cold of the snow.

A while passed with no words. He kicked a stone on the floor which got trapped between two cobbles and refused to jump anymore. Out of the blue, Oskar stopped in his tracks.

"Hana, if I don't do this now, I am really going to regret it."

All of a sudden, he let go of my hand to grab my waist and push me onto the wall, pressing out bodies together as his lips came crashing down onto mine.

I gasped, caught completely off guard.

He was kissing me. Oskar Diedrich was kissing me.

His hand travelled from my waist to my wrist, pinning it above my head in one harsh movement. I found myself kissing him back with equal passion, despite the lack of experience. He dominated the kiss and I let myself fall into his hands as our bodies mounded against each other with ravenous force.

He wasn't gentle.

His mouth was hot, wild and passionate.

I ignored the sting of my body against the rough wall, indulging in the scent of musk and savouring the taste of his sweet lips. A low growl emanated from the back of his throat as his tongue delved into my mouth, pushing my head against the wall behind me even harder.

Taken by complete surprise, I had dropped the bag of vinyls long ago. A parade was going off in my stomach every second my skin was in contact with his. My hands reached up and knocked the peaked hat off his head as my fingers intertwined themselves in his viciously dark hair, earning another breathy moan from him.

When he pulled away, I was gasping for air after he had knocked all the oxygen out of my lungs. He smoothed his hair down before picking up his hat and putting it on, as well as taking the bag of vinyls. He casually continued to walk down the cobbled path, a helpless grin on his face.

What on earth just happened?

Hoisting myself off the wall, I went to catch up with him. My mind was swimming with thoughts. Lots and lots and lots of thoughts.

Why did he kiss me? Why did I kiss him back? Why did I enjoy it?

"Where in Germany are you from?" He asked, out of nowhere. I wasn't sure why he was asking. It was an easy question but it felt so much more complicated now. My brain had retired from full consciousness after what he just did.

"Right here, in Berlin."

"Charlottenburg?" I involuntarily scoffed, unable to picture myself living my day to day life in such a posh and opulent area. Today was the first time I had step foot in the borough and I knew well enough that it was far too fancy for me.

"Oh, no. Kreuzberg. Very working class."

He scrunched up his nose. "Sounds awful."

"Actually, it wasn't so bad." I found myself innately smiling at the memory of my childhood. "Well, I mean, the air was. And most of the people. But it was home. I still know the place like the back of my hand."

"We could run away." He stopped walking and faced me. "No one would know. We can take your sister and we will be on the first train to Switzerland. You still have time."

I was finding it difficult to process what he was saying. Running away. Switzerland. I swallowed down the lump in my throat before I replied.

"I couldn't." My voice was shaking. "I'm not brace enough or strong enough. I could never do it."

At the first sight of a soldier, I would tremble. Escaping was too much for me, especially with Lola. I had never even been out of Germany before. It was overwhelming to think about running away. I couldn't. I just couldn't. Him by my side would only make it riskier. He had his duties and his responsibilities here which I could not get in the way of or else it would put me and Lola on even more danger.

"You are strong enough. But you're stronger without me." His palm pressed against my cheek, lifting my face until his eyes were locked with mine. "So when I say I will run away with you, what I'm really trying to say is that I will help you and Lola escape I'll give you money and a place to live and then you can find a man who actually deserves you that can look after you when you are not feeling so strong. It could work."

My airway felt tight. Maybe it was possible when my mother was still alive and when I could actually see myself leaving the electrified gates of the camps, but not now. All I had was Lola and if I lost her because I became too involved with escaping, I could never live with myself.

I didn't have the courage my mother had that she made seem completely effortless. I would see the beaming lights by the gates and cowardly retreat to the camps before I could even take a step out. If I saw an SS officer on the street, I would fall apart in bursts of tears and would completely blow my cover before he would even detect that I was a fugitive.

"It's too risky. I can't."

He let out a heavy sigh, throwing an arm around my shoulders and drawing me into his warmth. I hugged myself, trying to preserve as much heat as possible within the blaring winds of December.

"Diedrich?" Came a familiar voice as we reached the end of the alleyway. Oskar's arm instantly dropped from my shoulders to his side.

"Klaus? What are you doing here?" He sounded flustered, scratching the nape of his neck, uncomfortably.

Klaus. The one who touched me. I fixed my eyes on the floor, not trying to catch his attention.

"I'm headed to the Chancellory. Isn't your father supposed to be there?"

"Oh, I'm not with him. I'm out with my sisters." Oskar cleared his throat, aware of the distress on my face.

What would Klaus think? First, Oskar protected me at his birthday party and now we were walking out of an alleyway in Berlin together when I was supposed to be locked up. He would definitely be suspicious.

When his eyes landed on me, I tensed. "You have another sister?"

He didn't remember me.

"No. She's my maid." Oskar corrected, relief washing over him. A heavy weight felt alleviated off my shoulders when I was affirmed of his lack of suspicion. Then, he cocked his head to the side and started closely examining my features.

"Have we met?" His eyes lit up with recognition, immediately making me feel wary once more. Before I could respond, Oskar answered first.

"No, she's new on the job." He nodded his head a little too fast. "Well, we should get going. My sisters, they are very impatient girls! See you around then."

"See you around, Oskar." With one more questioning glance, Klaus walked away with, to my relief, no more questions. Thank god.

"It's okay, he was too drunk to remember." Oskar watched as Klaus walked away before walking back to the boutique. "Come on, let's get back."

The girls were still very preoccupied with their shopping, scavenging for the perfect dress. The exhausted personal shopper was sat on the sofa bundles of fabric and a tape measure around her neck.

"Are we ready to leave?" Oskar announced his presence, catching the girls attention. Ada and Carolina nodded but Elsa slumped onto the floor with her arms crossed over chest, her depressed eyes glued to the floor. "Elsa, what's the matter?"

"I don't have anything!" She whined, burying her head in her arms.

"What? You have been shopping for hours and you didn't find anything?" Oscar crouched to her level, placing a hand over her shoulder.

"I found one dress but Ada said I looked fat!" The little girl leaped up and charged towards her sister, punching her in the stomach. Adalina barely flinched at the light impact.

"Try it on and we'll see."

I zipped up her dress and watched her through the mirror as she examined the fit of it. She did not look fat at all. The dress looked as though it had been crafted by the hands of Fairy Godmother herself by the way it played with her youth and inspired regality in a young child.

"You look like a princess." Oskar kneeled by his sister, smiling at her natural beauty through the mirror. "You know what princesses need?"

"A tiara!" Elsa beamed, a giddy smile overtaking the disheartened expression she just held.

In that small moment of affection, I saw the human in his eye he was so scared to show the rest of the world, hidden beneath the patriotism and violence. Maybe he wasn't so bad, after all.

"Yeah, but not today. It's getting late." She nodded. "Ada, Carolina, did you manage to get more?"

"Adalina has selected seven from our range, and Carolina, thirty-eight." The drained shop assistant read out.

Thirty-eight? For a quiet girl, she really knew how to shop.

Oskar went ahead and wrote a cheque for an unspeakably large sum of money, before ushering them all out of the store.

"You would look beautiful in one of these dresses." He whispered by my ear, holding the door open for me.

I bit my lip, holding back a smile as I recalled what happened a little while ago over and over and over again in my mind.

He kissed me. He kissed me. He kissed me.

And I kissed him back.

Chapter 10

What happened yesterday never left my mind.

He expressed his affection towards me and I did not fight it. If anything, I provoked it even more. I let him press his body against mine and I let his long-caged ferocity unleash upon my lips.

It didn't mean that it was a bad thing, though. For my first (voluntary) kiss, it felt incredible. And even though I equalled his passion in the act, it did not necessarily mean that I equalled his feelings if he had felt any at all.

Heading back to the camps, I wrapped my arms tightly around my chest with a conventionally fuzzy feeling circulating around my body. I followed the soft glow of the sunset, muted by the thickening clouds but it still, somewhat, managed to penetrate through.

I was excited to see Lola. I didn't tell her about what happened but it felt good to know that I still had a piece of my old life left. I watched, this morning, as Elsa cried in Oskar's arms when it was time for them to leave and clung onto him despite her mother's stern protests. She was resistant to leave him and was only persuaded when he promised to visit her again, soon.

I did not know what it would feel like to lose Lola. We were always very close as sisters. We shared a bedroom and secrets and stories about school despite our ten year age gap and we had never spent a night apart. I cherished our relationship and she was always at the forefront of all my concerns.

When I reached my allocated cabin, a silent dread filled my lungs as the unsteady-looking wooden huts guarded by brute men materialised in my vision.

I walked past the soldiers with my head down, trying to pretend that they were not there at all as I reached for the handle of the gate.

Chatter died down when I entered, until an unhinging silence befriended the coldness of the poorly insulated room. Something felt off in the air. It made me shiver. It made me wonder why I was receiving such piercing glares from the women crowded in the small room.

Aware of the strange abundance of eyes fixated on my every move, I cautiously walked towards my usual bunk. When my eyes caught sight of Lola, I felt a twinge in my heart at the bundle of nervousness crouched into the corner of our shared bed.

"What's wrong?" I turned to the other prisoners, all of whom now held an expression of pure anger and resentment. Towards me?

"Whore!" A tug on my arm caused me to stumble back, just missing a swing to my face. I almost fell on top of Lola, who was tearing up as she let go of her grasp on my wrist.

"I- I don't understand." I stuttered, looking back and forth from my worried sister to the furious gang of women.

"Sleeping with the Commandant's son for preferential treatment?" Another woman growled, violently tugging a lock of my hair. "You little whore!"

I fell back on the mattress, speechless. Looking around at the masses of seething women, I gulped. Their boiling blood suddenly made the room rise a thousand degrees in temperature, leaving me immobile.

"I'm not sleeping with him! It's not like that" I defended, using all my lung-power. Lola had streams of tears running down her face as she gave me a look of concern.

"Liar!" A harsh strike to my face prevented me from seeing who said that. A sharp sting permeated through the side of my face. My eyes began welling with tears.

"Eloise works in the kitchen. She saw you and the Reichsführer's son on Christmas Day."

Mouth agape, realisation dawned on me.

She saw. She saw Oskar feeding me that truffle. She saw his arm around my waist when he did it. She saw me let it all happen!

"It's not what you think! I'm not sleeping with him, I swear!"

I knew it didn't sound convincing. I was only making matters worse. They were infuriated and I was helpless. I was in for trouble.

"You traitor! You selfish bitch!" Between their screamed insults, I heard Lola lightly sobbing behind me. I didn't know what to do.

"I heard he took her to Berlin!"

"Pretty face; of course she was going to use it to seduce the Reichsführer's son. That's what sluts like her do!"

What hurt most was not what they were saying, but the fact that it was all true.

I was a traitor. Lola and I had been getting extra food and he was undeniably lenient with me. I never did anything to stop him from getting close to me even if it was out of my control. Whether it was because I was scared of him or because I did not mind, it didn't matter. Their perceptions were set.

Their degrading words kept coming. I was barricaded between enflamed women, eager to burn me to the ground.

"In your beds, now!" A gruff voice from the door diverted everyone's attention.

Two SS soldiers had their rifles up, ready to diffuse the commotion using any means necessary. Instantaneously, everyone scurried into their bunks like children being told off by their mother at bedtime, all screams being muted. Relief washed over me as I tucked myself in next to Lola, avoiding eye contact with everyone.

"If I hear another sound, you won't see the sun rise again." The armed officers then exited, leaving the room swimming in a cold, violent stillness.

Moments passed and the aggressive stares remained. I turned to Lola, wiping the tears from her cheek with my sleeve.

"Why are you sleeping with him?" She asked, almost sounding hurt. "Don't you like sleeping next to me anymore?"

"Hey, hey," I whispered, pulling her into my arms. "It's not like that. I am not sleeping with anyone."

"Promise?" Her doe eyes glistened with her tears.

"I promise." I kissed the top of her head and stroked my hair until sleep had claimed her and soon after it had taken me too.

-

Thursday.

Thursdays were spent shooting, for Oskar.

I managed to convince Matron that Oskar had wanted to see me and was rather surprised when she did not see through my blatant lie.

When I usually would have been scrubbing his floors, I went to see him by the open field instead. He was alone, as he preferred to be, a raised gun in one hand pointing towards an array of targets twenty to twenty-five metres away. He was not wearing any safety equipment, just in his usual uniform.

Well concentrated, he was motionless. The material of his blazer was tight around the muscles of his arms. Minuscule waves were noticeable as he adjusted his position. I watched as he pulled the trigger several times, setting off a stream of bullets towards the targets, each hitting bullseye. He didn't flinch in the slightest.

The loud 'bang' caught me off guard, making me jump. Almost seeming startled, he turned around and saw me, hands pressed against my ears.

"Hana? What are you doing here?" He smiled, coming over to me and pulling my hands away from the side of my head.

"My head is ringing! How can you stand that loud noise?" It was dizzying, but he was unfazed.

"You get used to it." Oskar shrugged, taking a sip of water. The water must have been spiked because soon after taking that sip, a sly smile perked up on his face. "Have you ever shot a gun before?"

"What do you think?" I retorted, straight away. My eyes were prepared to fall out of my skull with disbelief when his arm extended out towards me, presenting his gun. "No!"

"Come on, it's fun!" He whinged, pulling my arm towards him when I attempted to back away.

Guns and I had a hate-hate relationship. I hated guns. I hated the word. I hated the sound it makes. I hated the damage it's done to me and I hated the destruction it could cause, any moment now.

"No, no, no!" I protested, shaking my head adamantly. It turned into muffles as his hand latched over my mouth, pulling me closer to his body.

"I'm not asking you anymore. I'm ordering you." His breath tickled my ear as he rested his chin on my shoulder.

His hand lowered from my mouth to my fists, opening it up and placing his reloaded gun into it with his other hand. My thumb traced the cold metal, the tactile feel of the various bumps and compartments unaccustomed to my touch.

His hand brushed over mine, moving my fingers into place. His touch was soft and measured. I felt his chest gently rise and fall against my back as he breathed. I felt unsure about this.

"Steady it with your hand." He directed in a low voice, pulling my arms up so the gun was pointing to the target. "Pull the trigger." His index finger wrapped over mine, contracting it to squeeze the trigger.

A sudden 'bang' blared into the air, making me jump. He steadied my body at the recoil, pressing me against him harder to stop me from falling.

It hit the target! Not bullseye, but close enough for a first try. I felt slightly proud of myself, I must admit.

When the temporary deafness subsided, I lowered my arms, taking in a deep breath. I stared at the impaled material, adrenaline pumping through my blood.

"How did that feel?" Registering his presence again, I swivelled around to return his gun.

"Exhilarating." I was grinning childishly.

I just shot a gun. Hana Amsel shot a gun. I even enjoyed it!

Maybe that was because my target was a just flimsy piece of painted cloth that didn't have a family or life.

"How does it feel when the target is a person?" I bit my cheeks, regretting what I just asked. I didn't want to know. What was I thinking?

"You want the honest truth?" He took a step back, slipping his gun back into his holster. I didn't move. "If a person deserves it... exhilarating."

My eyes travelled back to his waist. I felt nauseous. How many people had he shot with that very gun?

I observed the Iron Cross on his chest and the Swastika on his arm. His hat bore the eagle insignia of the Schutzstaffel, to represent what? Bravery? Propriety? Strength?

It reminded me why I came here to see him in the first place.

"You didn't tell me why you came to see me."

But I didn't possess the bravery to act with propriety and tell him what he stood for was depraved, so I simply said, "I forgot," and followed him back to his house.

When we got to his room, he put on a vinyl and sat me down next to him. I wanted to crawl away and not bear witness to his uncharacteristic yet recently more common tenderness. "What's wrong?"

The women were right to hurt me last night. I was fooling myself into thinking Oskar and I shared a mutual liking. It was him who directed the ostracism of so many innocent people of my kind. This was all just wrong.

I knew there was good in him, but it was not for me to possess. Whether I did it consciously or not, I was benefiting materially by his fondness for me and the moral weight had dropped on me yesterday when my fellow prisoners spoke up.

"I can't do this anymore." I huffed. "You have to stop."

Puzzled, he stood up. "What are you on about?"

"You know exactly what I am on about." My words came out strained but they had to be said. "Please."

His face dropped. He started pacing around the room. I watched, unable to move until I got an answer. Then, he stopped and was looking out of the window, tapping his foot, restlessly.

"Hana, have you ever loved anyone before?"

Oh god, this was bad.

He didn't mean what he said... Of course not.

He doesn't love you. You're deluded. He is just messing with your head!

"No, not romantically but –"

"Not romantically. Any type of love." His head snapped round. His dark eyes bore into mine, laced with suppressed anger.

"Well, yes."

"And if someone just came up and told you that you shouldn't love them anymore, could you?"

I thought about my parents and my sister. I didn't even have the option to not love them anymore. My parents were stripped away but they, as well as my sister, would always have an eternal stronghold in my heart.

I shook my head. For a while, he didn't say anything.

"You're dismissed for the day." He announced, cool and composed. Too cool and composed, like an iceberg dropped in a volcano.

"But –"

"Out. Now." I sensed the anger in his tone and didn't try to question him again. I left the room and headed downstairs, unable to process anything that had just happened.

When I got downstairs, the Reichsführer was busy at work with a cluster of documents spread across the living room coffee table. I did my best to remain undetected as I tiptoed passed the door, but the single creaky wood panel I just so happened to step on had other plans.

The Reichsführer's head shot up, looking rather annoyed. Panic-stricken, I froze.

"You there." I assumed he was referring to me as he collected his files. "Tell my son to see me in my office, immediately. Bring up some brandy whilst you're at it."

"Right away, Reichsführer." I responded, bowing my head. The man was stern and intimidating enough to head a school of delinquents. He could frighten an entire nation into subservience if he wanted to!

I ran upstairs as soon as I was out of his sight and knocked on Oskar's door.

"I'm busy." He responded, curtly.

"The Reichsführer wants to see you in his office, immediately." I replied through the door, nonetheless. He remained silent.

He was being stubborn and childish. I wasn't going to put up with it today. I would, tomorrow, when I have had some time to clear out my mind and fully understand what on earth is going on. Today, passivity was my friend.

I sprinted to the basement and grabbed a bottle of brandy, aware of the impatience of the great Reichsführer. When I entered his office, I immediately noticed the friction between Oskar and his father. He was sat down at his desk whilst his son was standing in from of him with the strictest posture, as if talking to a leading Nazi and not just his father.

I paid no attention, respecting their privacy and went straight ahead to place the brandy at the Reichsführer's desk, filling up a glass for him. I was eager to leave.

I turned around to head out of the door until Reichsführer's eyes landed on me, sending a chill up my spine. He narrowed his eyes, leaning forward in his chair with a dark air of authority.

"You. Stay."

Chapter 11

I gulped.

The Reichsführer's sharp stare burned through my skin. I straightened my back and lowered my head, trying to seem as unnoticeable as possible.

It was fine. He probably just wanted someone to refill his drink every so often and I was the most convenient person to do that. I was just overthinking.

"Do you know why I called you here?" The Commandant asked his son, taking a sip of brandy. Oskar hesitated, looking to me quickly with a faint stab of pain in his eyes.

"No, Reichsführer." He looked puzzled, playing with his fingers behind his back as he stood opposite his father. His father leaned back on his chair, resting one hand on top of the other on the edge of his desk, tilting his head to the side with an unamused scowl.

"Then maybe Hana, here, could care to explain."

My stomach knotted up.

It had to be a coincidence that he knew my name. A pure, unimaginably peculiar coincidence.

He, like his ex-wife, must have heard Oskar call me by my name in some odd circumstance. Probably the same dinner, even. Although it was known of the Reichsführer having a lack of attention when it came to knowing the names of his household staff, it was the only reasonable explanation.

"I- I'm not sure what you mean, Reichsführer." I stammered, my voice coming out small.

"Oh, I think you know exactly what I mean." He chuckled like it was the most humorous thing in the world.

"Father, what's going on?" Oskar looked from his father to me, cautiously.

"Do you know how much it embarrasses me to find out that my only son is romantically interested in his maid?" His haughty laugh echoed through the frigid room. "Oh, and not just any old maid! A prisoner of his own camp, no less!"

My jaw fell.

Anxiety racked up in my stomach, toying with my breathing and forming goosebumps on my arms. Oskar shared the same, dreadful expression.

"I have no idea what you're talking about." He spurted out, confidently folding his arms over his chest. He was shaking on the inside, I knew. He was just more trained than me in concealing it.

"Don't play with me, boy!" He yelled, rising from his chair with austerity. "Have you been sleeping with her or not?"

"That's not something I'm comfortable discussing with you." He swallowed, watching his father, attentively.

"I don't care." Reichsführer gritted his teeth, walking around the desk to face his son. "Answer my question."

"So what if I am sleeping with the help? Why is it suddenly a problem for you now?"

I wanted to scream that we were not sleeping together. It had barely been ten minutes since I sincerely broke off whatever we had, which most definitely did not constitute to sex.

Then again, he was being very tactful.

By outwardly denying any amorous feelings, his father would only assume that he is lying, which would only dig our graves deeper. It was smart to illustrate it as a petty liaison, something any man in the Reichsführer's status would probably not have any concern with.

Only, he did not buy it.

"This isn't about sleeping with the help. This is about falling in love with a criminal!" He turned his back to Oskar as his fist came crashing down the empty desk. The impact vibrated across the room, making me jump.

I hugged my chest, holding back the tears of fear straining to be released.

"I am not in love with her!" Oskar protested, fiercely.

The Commandant's head gradually turned towards me, looking immensely agitated. In measured strides, he advanced towards me and took a fistful of the flimsy material of my dress.

"Where's her triangle?" Reichsführer seethed, glowering at Oskar.

His height and build loomed over me, like an eagle upon its prey. I remained fixated on the wood of the floor, submerged in the aura of his authoritarian grandeur and his naturally exuding threat.

Oskar remained silent. It was the smartest thing to do.

Oskar's father walked over to him, dropping a hand on his shoulder. "You have disappointed me so much. I am so ashamed to call you my son."

"I haven't done anything wrong." He scoffed, sounding strained. "It's not even illegal. She is not a Jew."

"She's manipulating you." Reichsführer scorned, staring intensely at Oskar. "She's using you. I thought you were smart enough not to fall for that."

My mouth hung open with shock. He was the one who used me. Manipulated me. Not the other way round!

"That's not true!" Oskar pushed the Reichsführer's hold off his shoulder. "You don't know the half of it."

His father sharpened his stare. "She has made you weak."

Biting my tongue, I let what he said surpass my mind. I was on the verge of exploding, nearing my final straw. Only, I couldn't imagine what I would do if he had pulled all my strings.

"It's not like that –"

He was the Commandant of the camp I was serving in. He was the head of the household I was slaving away at. He could snap my neck and have me dead in an instance with no one to question him.

"Then prove to me she has not weakened you."

At the clap of his hands, two colossal SS men stormed through the double doors, lugging a four-foot tall, striped uniformed and chestnut haired girl by her arms between them.

Lola.

In that moment, I felt the world around me start spinning at a sickening speed as I witnessed all the family I had left be dragged into a room full of ruthless soldiers. Anger transformed into a monster of distress.

They pushed her to her knees as she looked around the unfamiliar room before her eyes landed on me. Paralysed, I simply stared at the lost girl, wishing this was all just a nightmare and that I would wake up soon.

"What's going on?" I choked out, panic-stricken. When my sight fell on the table, I was ready to fall myself.

A gun.

I couldn't think straight. A gun. My sister. Then prove to me she has not weakened you.

"Kill her." Reichsführer demanded, setting off a tornado of concern in my head.

I didn't even register his words at first. Kill her. Kill her. Kill her. Kill Lola. Kill my sister.

"Father, please." To my relief, Oskar did not move. "She's just a little girl."

Relief? Relief was long gone now.

"So what if she is just a little girl? Why is it suddenly a problem for you now?" He asked, smug, echoing Oskar's earlier words.

"No, no, please! She hasn't done anything wrong!" I clutched my hands, begging to spare her life but my cried were muffled by their silence.

"Hana, what's happening?" Lola frowned, her arms still hoisted up by the two men on either side of her. Naivety was the only blessing bestowed upon her, in this moment.

"How did you even know about us?" Oskar asked, forcefully looking away from me and my visibly frightened sister.

The girls in the camp.

They must have told someone who informed him. This is how they chose to take their spite out on me. With my life and the life of an innocent other.

"It seems Oberführer Haas' son is more inclined to national duty than his personal relations, unlike you."

I scoured my memory, the name meaning nothing to me. It left me more worried than before.

Then, Oskar's hands formed fists at his side. "Klaus."

I looked down to Lola, who seemed overly fascinated by a ladybird crawling across the floor. She was living in her head, away from this torturous confrontation in a land where people like the Reichsführer did not exists.

"I'm not going to kill her." Even at Oskar's statement, I did not feel settled. He only proved his father's theory.

"Hana, am I going to die?"

My breathing became laboured at the weights sitting in my lungs. It all felt unreal. Part of me was still hoping it wasn't Lola pushed on the floor but just my imagination.

"Okay. New game." The Reichsführer sneered, picking up the gun for himself. "One of them dies. You choose."

Horror surged through my veins. Just when I thought there was a chance for Lola, I was faced with this ultimatum that was mandated by Oskar's impulse. I knew which way he would sway.

But I couldn't let my sister suffer the consequences of my mistakes.

"Kill me. Me. Please." I fell to my knees before Oskar, pleading for him to spare my sister. "She hasn't done anything wrong. Let her live, I'm begging you!"

"Hana, don't." He pushed me away and leaned against the wall. "If they kill you, they will kill her anyways."

All oxygen was snatched away from my lungs, replaced by an aching pain that was tearing me apart.

She could die. It wasn't fair. She had only seen the world for a mere six years. She had yet to finish school, to build a career, to fall in love. She had her entire life ahead of her.

"Well, son. Who's it going to be?"

Oskar looked to everyone and everything in the room but me. When I pulled his hand into mine, he tugged it away and shook his head.

"If you really do love me, you'll choose me."

"Just hold her, Hana." He ran a hand through his hair, leaving me cold and dry and dying in a state of shock. Reichsführer smiled at his choice.

Hesitating, I crawled over to Lola. Her eyelids drooped down, heavy with tiredness. Her cheek bones prodded out after months of malnutrition and labour. Waves of unkempt chocolate hair fell down the front of her face, concealing her youthful innocent and beauty.

I pulled her shoulders towards me, wrapping my arms around her and holding her as tight as humanly possible. Water from my eyes dampened her hair as tears came out in waterfalls. Her silk cheeks pressed against my neck as I kept her enclosed in my embrace, savouring every second she was in my arms.

I pulled back, slightly, hovering my lips above her ear. I whispered, "Close your eyes and count to ten, like when we were home and used to play Hide and Seek. Go on."

Iron bars that caged my heart contracted, agonisingly relentless.

"Ten, nine..."

I rushed over to Oskar, wailing in the presence of my sister, who was absentmindedly counting away, in a final attempt to free her from this treacherous fate.

"Please, Oskar. Please don't do this. She doesn't deserve this. Please."

"Eight, seven..."

He turned away and closed his eyes shut, cowardly hiding away in his mind. Reichsführer picked up the gun, loading it in a skilled movement.

"Six, five..."

Lola and I used to play Hide and Seek all the time. Her favourite hiding spot was in the laundry basket, much to Mama's disfavour. I would usually be the one seeking, since she often felt humiliated if she forgot the number seven when counting. When she had finally gotten all the numbers correct, she would never let me be the seeker to proudly show off her newfound skill.

"Four, thr –"

'BANG'

"You shouldn't let someone you love count up to their deaths, Hana."

The entire universe came to a grinding halt around me. Everything was still.

I was still. Oskar was still. The gun held up in his father's hand was still, except for the faint trail of smoke that was calmly dancing out from the end of it.

Lola was still.

Her body lay soundless on the floor, blood oozing out of the perfect circle incised on the side of her head, where the bullet had seared through. The red liquid pooled around her, staining her paled skin and fortifying the notion of her death.

Distress shook me to the very core, abandoning me in a volcano of numbness as I sat there, staring at the breathless body of my murdered sister, wondering what she had done so wrong in her life to deserve this end.

Chapter 12

- -

An hour later, I was still hanging over my stone cold sister, still unable to shed a single tear.

"Come on, Hana. Get up." Oskar pressed, gently dropping a hand on my shoulder which I was quick to shove off.

"Don't touch me." I growled through gritted teeth. His touch felt almost as painful as the bullet that had just gone through my sister, only the deep mark it left was imprinted in the inside of my head rather than through it.

"Hana –"

"I don't care."

My laboured breaths echoed in hiccups of cries as I clutched Lola's limp shoulder, trying to force her back to life but it wasn't working.

Nothing I did could rejuvenate her back to the lovely child she was. She was stone cold as her spirit escaped her, leaving a greying wake in its path.

Dead.

My sister was dead.

"Hana, stand up." I didn't register what he was saying as my insides stirred with disbelief. I held her tighter to me. "Hana, get up now. That's an order."

I couldn't think straight. Words were not coming to my mouth. Strength was not coming to my bones. When he grasped my arm and forced me up, I did not have the energy to stop him, so I let him drag me away from my sister as my eyes remained fixated on the direction of her resting body, numb to the world.

By the time he had hauled me to the cabins, I felt more weak and limp than ever. When his hand let go of my arm, my shoulders sank and my knees felt like liquid as I pressed myself against the wood of the walls, trying to keep myself up.

"I'm sorry." He muttered, twisting his foot in the thick snow to make a small hole. The lamps dropped a yellow glow over his face where there was no shadow, flickering restlessly as he eyed the indent his shoes made in the snow. "I know it won't change anything, but I really am."

Lola was dead and what did he care? He could have stopped it but he chose not to. When the life of all the family I had remaining sat at the mercy of his hands, he discarded it nonchalantly like lint he just picked off his coat.

"And if someone just came up and told you that you shouldn't love them anymore, could you?"

Liar.

If he could drop love in a second, he definitely had not felt it at all.

"What if it was Elsa?" The question came out sharp and hit him hard, almost like a bullet to the head.

He swallowed cautiously, stuffing his hands in his pockets. "I don't understand your question."

"What if it was your sister in Lola's position? You would never have let her die like that!" I found myself shouting with all the power vested in my lungs, which was not enough to make it more than a screech. Against the subzero temperature, I was boiling. Fuming. Burning with rage.

"I said I'm sorry."

"And I said 'I don't care'." I growled, clutching my turbulent stomach with one hand before grasping the handle of the door with the other. "Goodnight, Herr Diedrich."

When I made it to my bunk, I ignored the searing stares stabbing at my presence. Instead, I silently fed myself into the side of the bed, which was already refilled with two newcomers.

Losing my family burned.

It stabbed a dagger in my chest and twisted it until all that was left was a tragic mess of bone splinters and decaying muscles. It left a harrowing wind slamming against my face every time I tried to stand up and threw me down to the ground with brute force to leave its mark. It wrapped around me like the packaging of a present but then the ribbons became too tight and the pressure became too unbearable until I was ready to combust.

Her blood was on my hands.

Had I not become involved with the camp commandant's son, none of this would ever have happened. Only I was to blame for her loss. I was to blame for her murder.

-

In the morning, I dreaded going back to work. It was one thing being in the Diedrich household and another working for Oskar Diedrich, himself.

But I chose to be professional, docile and silent.

If he would ask me to do anything, I would do it straight away without question. If he needed anything, I would retrieve it as quickly as possible. I would assume the role of an efficient and reliable maid, just as I was expected to be.

No preferential treatment, no superfluous conversation, no out of line interaction with Herr Diedrich.

If he worked me until my blood became dry, so be it. I wasn't there by choice. I was there for slave labour and protesting would only make matters worse.

From now on, I would do my job and that would be all.

When I got to the gates of the house, I was met by two soldiers guarding the entrance. I became accustomed to the imposing glares and the gun filled hands, only I felt slightly more apprehensive today.

Probably because as soon as I appeared, they held up the rifles in their hands towards me.

"W-what's going on?" I choked out, grabbing a fistful of my uniform, absentmindedly.

"You are no longer permitted on these premises." Almost robotically, one of the men answered.

"I don't understand. I work for Herr Diedrich." The guns filled me with dread. They weren't similar to the ones that killed my sister, but the mere thought of what it could do was scarring.

"Reichsführer's orders. You are to go back to your previous work timetable."

I let out an exasperated sigh as I turned back round to the long path back
to the camps. I was back to the routine shovelling and labouring. Maybe it
was a good thing.

No more drama. No more accusations. No more Oskar Diedrich.

That was only for a split second until, half way to my destination, two
clammy hands clasped my wrists and started dragging me elsewhere.

I writhed in their iron hold, jutting my legs around maniacally as I was
lifted off the ground.

"What are you doing?" I yelled, slamming my arms around but my attempt
to be released was futile. Their grasps tightened alongside their steeled
faces, until we reached the opening of some trees, where they dropped me
to the ground.

The mess of rocks on the ground stung the palm of my hands and my
kneecaps. I hissed at the sudden burst of pain, rubbing my palms together
to try and ease the burning sensation.

"Stand up."

The familiar cold voice sent a tornado of trepidation zipping through my
body.

No. Not again.

Warily, I raised my head to come eye to eye, once more, with Reichsführer
Diedrich.

Stood beside him, with a look of shock overloaded on his face, was his son.

Once again, I started praying that the earth would be merciful and devour
me instantly to free me from all this torture.

Instead, the ground remained solid and held me up as I pushed myself off it to stand. My stomach churned and my joints were on the verge of snapping, contrary to the Diedrichs' composure and high and mighty disposition.

"Are you going to kill me?" The hem of my dress had hitched up when I fell, so I pretended to seem preoccupied with that, pulling it down and not looking towards the two.

"Father, what is she doing here?" Concern leathered his tone, but I knew better than to believe Herr Diedrich possessed the slightest bit of selflessness.

I didn't care anymore.

He could kill me.

What did I have to lose?

A gap between some trees formed the space of land. Looming branches curtained the sunlight but was not agile enough to stop slithers of light from peeking through.

When enough courage had built up in me to look directly at the murderer of my sister, I regretted it immediately when I saw the conniving smugness that permeated from his grin.

"Beat her."

His order to his son was spoken in a low, measured tone. Though it was unmistakable what he said, the words were playing on a loop in my head as I tried to comprehend what he was saying.

Herr Diedrich's mouth dropped. He didn't move. "No."

"Now, Oskar. Don't make me tell you again."

Keeping a straight face, I waited patiently. I was tired and drowsy and ready to fall apart at the seams.

Oskar stood defensively. "I won't don't it. I won't."

The silver ornaments on his uniform glistened under the minimal streaks of sunlight, mocking his refusal to follow his father's command. Reichsführer seemed unbearably unsatisfied as his eyes turned red and he clenched his jaw.

"Either do it now, or I will have your mother arrested. You wouldn't like that, now would you?"

I didn't understand that statement. What could his mother be arrested for? Nonetheless, it seemed to click something in him. Something big. A grave look shadowed over Herr Diedrich as he looked from his father to me.

"Why are you doing this?" In a strained voice, he asked his father. I wanted to know the same. I had done nothing wrong. I had lost so much. Why was he doing this?

"To make sure you are still at least half the man you were before you fell in love with her."

Herr Diedrich shook his head, disbelievingly. This wasn't fair. Why was I the one suffering for his weaknesses?

"I'm so sorry, Hana. I didn't want to do this." He sounded apologetic as he gradually approaching me. "I care about you, a lot. But my family comes first. I'm sorry."

I had not cried since my sister died. That's why it came to me as such a surprise when dampness started fogging my sight now.

When I was a little girl, I wanted to be a nurse, just like my mother. I wanted to help people and silently make a difference in someone's life, as boring as it sounds. By now, I would have hoped to finish school and fall in love and help Lola with her German homework.

Instead, I had lost all the dignity I once obtained and possessed the value of less than an animal. No one was left in the world for me. Nothing was left for the universe to give. My own name did not even mean anything to me anymore.

"Okay." I murmured, bracing myself.

He took his time making his way over, unable to look me in the eye as he did so. He halted a mere foot away from me, offering a final apologetic frown.

The first blow came as a kick to my abdomen. I was a very fragile person and the impact left a stabbing pain to domineer its way through my body. I grunted at the force, falling victim to the power of a ravenous animal. I did not think a person could have so much strength to have me crouching with my arms tied around my midriff, begging for the ache to stop.

Then, there came the uncomfortable sound of skin smacking skin as his fist met my jaw, propelling me straight to the ground. My vision became blurry and my head began to spin, but for what felt like years, I let the blows and bruises come freely, until the Reichsführer had decided he was satisfied with his son's work and I was left on the ground in a hazy daze, tilting between consciousness and a morbid darkness, desperate for the ground to offer me some solace.

Chapter 13

- -

"**A**re you here to gloat?"

Hans leaned against the doorframe of the infirmary room, looking down on me as I finished redoing the bandages on my left hand.

"No." He sounded sincere. He sat down opposite me and presented a neatly wrapped package. "I brought you something to eat."

I suppose I should be hungry, since I had spent the night in the infirmary trying to recollect myself without a bite to eat. Only, I found that my appetite was non-existent and the thought of food made me feel nauseous.

Swiftly undoing the tie of the bag, a brief look of concern flashed through his eyes as they caught sight of my injured face. I turned my head away to avoid his blatant pity, which only caused a sharp sting to strike through my neck.

"Try not to move too much." Hans advised, resting a hand on my cheek lightly to turn my head to face him. His glistening eyes scoured mine, momentarily falling on my bandaged wrist resting on my lap and then my other arm that was tightly holding my throbbing abdomen. "I can't believe he did this to you."

"Yes, you can." I huffed, leaning back on the chair. "You were the one that warned me about it."

Maybe if I had listened to him, none of this would have ever happened.

I felt awful.

He was just trying to be a decent friend and look out for me. I threw it back in his face and now I was suffering the tremendous consequences. I felt awful. Awful and foolish. My naivety led to the downfall of all my family and now there was nothing left that I could do to change it back.

"I am so sorry that I didn't listen to you before, Hans. I am."

"Don't mention that anymore. I'm just glad you are alive, right now."

The warmth of his smile filled up the whole room, bringing ease to my jittery self and making me really appreciate his company.

The room bathed in the sharp smell of antiseptic and drying blood as the common buzz of overworked and abused prisoners being admitted and discharged faded into the distance. A gratifying silence blanketed the prior conversation as I delved into the part of my mind that would not stop dwelling on how awful my life had turned out. It made me want to fall to my knees and burst out crying.

"You should run."

"Huh?" So entranced with my thoughts, I barely registered what Hans was saying.

"Escape, I mean." He stated, in a hushed voice. "Its your only way out of here. You can do it. I can help you."

Blinking hard once, I attempted to process his suggestion. His ridiculously ludicrous suggestion, that was, that I was hearing for the second time this week.

"No way." I scoffed, disbelieving to his seriousness on the matter. "That's for people who aren't scared of tiny insects and harmless, inconspicuous noises. Not me."

"You can, Hana." Hans stressed, as if it were that easy. "There's a five minute gap in the electrifications every night. It's a straight road out from here and I can give you some food and money to last you a few days. It could work."

Ignoring the growing headache, I shook my head, affirmatively. "No, Hans. No, it couldn't. Stop being ridiculous."

He sighed, heavily, giving up. "Matron told me to tell you that the Reichs-führer wants you back to work, immediately." He stood up and turned towards the exit after gesturing to the items he left for me. "Make sure you get some food in you before you leave."

Throwing me a small smile, he left the building with a faint look of disap-pointment lingering off him.

Running away would be impossible.

I was a weak person, admittedly. Nothing in me would find the strength to fight to death for my freedom, even without Lola as a responsibility. I would cower at the first sight of threat faster than anyone can imagine.

Drawing together all the little strength in my bones, I hauled myself up and out of the infirmary, desperate to not cross paths with the Reichsführer again. It would be easier now that Herr Diedrich and I would be complete-ly apart. I just had to do my work well, for the time being, and maybe one day I would pluck up the courage to escape into a better part of the world.

Heading for the sorting station, I often caught staring eyes stuck on me. On my busted up face. On the way I limped when I tried to walk.

Paying no mind to them, I continued advancing to the station, desperate to get my mind off of anything Oskar Diedrich.

That was, all until a cold metal object slammed against my head with a ferocious force, instantly knocking me out.

-

My eyelids fluttered open, met with the damp bark and icy air amongst imposing pillars. The majority of these were familiar, stagnant trees that served as a reminder of how small we were as people. Two were uniformed and armed men whom I had not encountered before, a hellish grin decorating both their faces.

I groaned, pressing a palm to my forehead which was swelling with agony. In a momentary lapse of dizziness, I pushed myself off my stomach, wincing at the immutable sting.

"Are you sure we are allowed to do this?" One voice came, echoing in my ears.

"Yes. Reichsführer Diedrich said we can do what we want with her, just not to kill her."

Dread pervaded my body, perfect company to the discomfort loosely holding together my bones.

"What's the point of that then?" He sounded disappointed.

"Who cares?"

As I lay on the floor, clutching my stomach and incapable of muttering any pleas for compassion, I felt the strong sole of a soldier's boot strike my hip with the sheer force of a gargantuan monster on steroids.

I cried out at the sudden burst of pain that came with a cracking sound, which was turned into muffles as another kick came to my face.

The men laughed sadistically at my torture, continuing to throw me around like a rag doll headed to the bins.

"What the hell do you think you're doing?"

The outraged voice created a small space of comfort in my chest, despite the growing discomfort all over my body.

"H-Herr Diedrich. W-we d-didn't know that –"

"Didn't know what?" He raised an eyebrow, draining the colour from the faces of the other SS men. When he caught sight of me on the floor, I closed my eyes tightly after seeing the sorrow expressed in him. "You two, leave."

Two sets of footsteps left the area. My vision was very blurry but I definitely noticed Herr Diedrich crouch down beside me.

"Let's get you out of here." He whispers, picking up my lesser injured arm and pulling it around his shoulders. The small action felt like my arm was ripping apart.

"Not so fast."

Oskar froze, dropping my arm back to my side and standing up straight. I stayed on the floor, unable to move, finally immune to the affliction these forests held.

"No, please. Just leave her alone. Please." Herr Diedrich begged, taking a step closer to his father.

"You would never have had a problem with a prisoner being beaten up before."

I lost balance on my side lying down on the floor, falling onto my back, causing agony to sear through me.

"Just this once, I'm asking you as your son. Doesn't that mean anything to you?"

"You may ask me as my son, but I am telling you as your Reichsführer that I will not tolerate your affection towards her. Understand?"

Maybe I ought to escape. Even if it all fails, dying out there would be so much better than dying in here.

"Beat her, again. Don't question me this time."

"She's weak enough. Please, father. Please."

"It's either her or your mother and sister. There is no third choice here."

Oskar went silent.

I twisted my head left and right, unable to find a comfortable position.

Then, I heard footsteps approach me.

"Hana, I'm –"

"Just do it. It's not like you don't have it in you."

I took in a deep breath and let it out again, like releasing an entrapped bird from its cage. I looked to the sky, where wondrous figures of white effortlessly danced through the blue, impervious to the notion of war and violence and adversity.

I noticed his hesitancy at first, but if he faltered in front of the Reichsführer, his flame would only be provoked more.

He commenced by kneeling beside me on the floor to get a close hit to my face with his fist. Instantaneously, stars started cropping up in my vision like in a surreal dream. My other cheek thrashed against the ground, grazed by the jagged bark covering the floor.

This time I wasn't shaking or trembling or remotely scared. I accepted what came with a forceful grace, pretending that I would wake up tomorrow and this would all be over.

I wheezed when he stabbed his foot into my abdomen, liquifying all my organs. He was stronger than the last two men combined, evident in the marks that he most probably left on my body.

The energy to register the pain drained away after a while.

I let the blows come and the rancid taste of death linger on my tongue. I let my eyelids fall, dreaming of the luxury that was sleep and wondering how many days it will be until I get it next.

In a momentary intermission between the chronic beating, my ears managed to pick up faint words being spoken through the grey screen over my vision.

"That's enough. She's unconscious."

"I shall be the one to make the decision of when enough is enough."

The torment resumed.

Soon after, numbness washed over my frail body, abandoning me in the shadow of blackness, mercy to the icy winds and iron fists of someone I thought I trusted.

•••

A/N

Combined two chapters in one for this and it slightly saddens me because it means the total number of chapters is no longer in the five times table.

Well, hope you enjoyed

(Cover in header by @QueenAmeythyst).

Chapter 14

- -

I woke up to find myself lying in an infirmary bed, covered in more bruises than I fell asleep with.

My battered body sunk into the worn mattress, accommodating my feather weight with distressed creaks and squeaks as I shifted to adjust my comfortability.

Only, comfortability was long gone.

I was drooping into an avalanche of malaise, after riding head-first into a sandstorm of soreness like a circus master being torn apart, limb by limb, by his aggravated lion.

My arms felt as though they had been aggressively torn off by a bullfighter only to be loosely stitched back to my shoulders by the bumbling hands of a blind grandmother. My legs felt like they had been mistaken for asphalt and had been ran over by an army tank, again and again. My swollen eyes blocked some of my vision and stung every time I blinked, worse than the last time I was here.

I started to remember why father said he used to drink.

"It helps to ease the pain, Hana. It helps to ease the pain." He would say, sullenly downing another bottle.

Maybe it could do the same for me.

Ignoring the growing cramps in my neck, I gradually turned my head to the side and glared at the silver hip flask being anxiously swirled around in Oskar's hand.

Crouched in the wooden chair, his dark hair was dishevelled and his blood-shot eyes were circled with dark bags as he was in deep thought. His hands hurriedly brought the flask to his lips as if some monstrous thought had just entered his mind that he was eager to flush out.

Then, through the corner of his eyes, he caught sight of me.

"You're awake!" He noticed, leaning forward with a grand look of relief. "You were out for almost three days."

I remained transfixed at the bottle in his hold.

"Oh," he whispered, noticing my fascination. He dark eyes flickered to mine and all in an instant, I realised how intoxicated he was. "Do you want some?"

Gently nodding, I let my lips part slightly as he brought the flask over to me, pressing the mouth against my lips and tilting it upwards to let the sharp liquid flow down my throat.

I relished in the fire it lit across my body, concocting warmth in all my insides and extremities, where all I had been feeling was the cold of the camps for the last few months.

He retracted sluggishly, taking a good look at every bruise and every cut he had implanted onto my body before taking his seat again. I remained indifferent under his long stare, numb to the calamity he could inflict.

"What did he mean when he said he would have your mother arrested?" I choked out, remembering his reaction to his father's threats.

The question caused him to cower for a moment as he fiddled with the cap of the flask in his hands. Soon after, in a drunken slur, he answered.

"My mother had an affair with a Russian spy in the last two years of their marriage. Elsa is the product."

Something in me clicked.

Rage started fuming in me as glared at the heartless hypocrite in front of me.

"You accused me of not being German enough, when your sister is half-Russian, your mother had an affair with one and you and your entire family are protecting them!" I was seething with rage, my bruised hands clenching tight by my waist as I narrowed my eyes at him, furious. "How dare you?"

He didn't have an answer.

He just started at the floor, impassively.

"You know what? You're just a coward." He looked at me again, confused. "You use girls because you are so self-superior. You are a drunkard who only drinks because you can't even be bothered to face reality and you are a soldier who is not even faithful to his own country! You don't even have the capacity to change. You are nothing but pathetic!"

"Hana, –"

"I don't care what you do to me for saying that. Rape me. Beat me. Kill me. You deserved to hear it."

"I'm not going to hurt you." He gently placed his hand over mine, but I jerked it away with lightning speed, ignoring the overly familiar sting.

"Don't touch me." I growled, through clenched teeth. He made me fume. His touch made me feel disgusting.

"I'm sorry, Hana." A lonely tear trailed down his cheek as his eyes pleaded to mine for some form of forgiveness.

Sorry wasn't going to bring my father back. Sorry wasn't going to bring my mother back. Sorry wasn't going to bring Lola back. Sorry wasn't even going to help me recover, so what was it even worth?

"I am a good person Oskar. I am." I strained. "I've never done anything bad in my life."

"I know that, Hana. I know, I know." He nodded his head, breathing heavily.

"I always see the best in people and I hate myself so much for only ever seeing the best in you, which is worth nothing compared to all the bad you have done."

It felt like a dagger was being repeatedly stabbed into my abdomen, each jab as bad as the last.

"I don't lie, I don't steal and I certainly do not kill, but I am the one lying in an infirmary bed whilst you get to live such a luxury life in a beautiful home with all your family safe, when you don't care about anyone but yourself! How is that fair?"

I started to sound like a crazy person. I had never been this angry before in my entire life. I needed an explanation. I needed a reason. I needed something, anything.

"It's not. I know it's not." He was crying more now, which I resented. Why was he allowed to be upset over my suffering? "You're a good person, Hana. The greatest. You deserved so much better."

"Did you ever even love me?"

He remained silent, leaving me in the dark.

I, too, became quiet after that. I knew better than to allow anger to hold a bearing over me in such a manner. After all, I was the better person.

A lot of time passed after my outburst. I was consumed with enmity, but it caused more pain to my joints and my wounds than it ever could to him. So, I remained silent, mentally jeering at my pathetic self and occasionally stealing sips from his silver hip flask.

He did not dare say anything either. He wept quietly, which, every so often, was promptly halted by a swing of liquor.

"I never wanted to hurt you," he let out, in what was almost a whisper.

I stopped fidgeting with the loose strings of the thin blanket and faced him, pushing my head off the pillow.

"I cared about you a lot." He looked down. "But I care about my family a lot, too. You understand what family means to a person, don't you?"

I sat up properly, leaning against the backboard of the bed for support. It felt like I was being torn in half, but the agony was only short-lived.

"This is how it was always meant to be. You are the one that is meant to hurt me."

In truth, whatever he had to say, I didn't care anymore.

"Hana," he pleaded. "I did care about you, I did. I promise."

I had never been a cynical person. I always saw the best in every situation. I found that that talent had escaped me right now, with only anger and resentment to take its place.

"The only reason we know each other is because of happenstance and coincidence!" The temper in my voice brought pain to my lungs. "We are from two entirely different worlds. We are at war with each other, for crying out loud! This was never supposed to happen!"

He gulped. "You're right. I'm sorry."

"I really hope you are."

Breathless, I remained sitting upright on the bed as only the alcohol provided decent company. Oskar was lost in thought, thoughts I did not care to hear.

When the agony was not too much to bear, I thought about how happy I was this time last year. There was no war, no conflict, no disaster.

Just me and my family in a small flat in Kreuzberg, constantly failing to light the fireplace properly.

And then totalitarianism and tyranny had to come along and steal that all from me. More violently and more heartlessly than I ever could have imagined.

"Will you help me to stand up?"

"Shouldn't you rest?" Sensing my annoyance, he stood up and wrapped an arm around my waist, hoisting me up to my feet. Feeling his skin against mine was not nice, but I swallowed down the repulsion nonetheless.

The movement was small but painful. I winced as all my weight was focussed on my injured legs. Unintentionally, I lurched forward, but his strong arm steadied me until I was standing firmly.

Cautiously, he took a single step back, observing my balance, or lack there-of. Closer up now, I took a better look at him.

He may not be a particularly good person, but he was definitely very handsome. The kind of guy girls fell for at first glance.

It was only after the first glance you would see the genocide and abuse and brutality instilled in his day to day motive. Nothing about him was sane or likeable. He was corrupt and depraved, stemming straight off from his father.

"I hate you. I hate you with every cell and bone and drop of blood in me and if that means you're going to kill me, go ahead. Kill me now. Do whatever the hell you want, I have nothing to lose."

"I am not going to hurt you."

I didn't believe that. He said he would not hurt me before, but here I was, wobbling as I tried to stand up straight. He would hurt me over and over again at the command of his father, or anyone else, perhaps. He lived under the illusion of concern, when really, he was just as bad as the rest of them.

Nothing was going to change anytime soon. He was a bad person, inside and out. There was no remedy or prayer in the world that could change a person of his nature into something that even slightly resembles good.

When my eyes flickered to his waist, I realised maybe there could be a way to end this cycle of torture, after all.

I lunged for his gun, ignoring the stabbing pains tearing apart my body. His hand grabbed my wrist, trying to push me away but my elbow jerked into his abdomen, causing a sting throughout my arm and temporary misdirection in him.

This is your chance.

Within a flash, I had the gun facing him.

A look of horror dropped over his face as he raised his hands up by his shoulders, eyes wide open.

"Hana, be careful with that." He insisted, cautiously trying to step closer to me. I jutted the gun forward, warning him off.

"You deserve this." If I was not so caught in the moment, I would have realised how painful my chest was with my increasingly heavy breathing. "You have killed so many people already."

"I know I do, Hana. But, I know you. You could never live with the guilt of killing someone." He stated, speaking each word slowly as though I were a child.

"But I would stop you hurting so many other people. So many other families."

I remembered that time I watched him shoot a gun before.

Turn off the safety.

"If you shoot me, someone will come in here and kill you instantly."

Steady it with your hands.

"I have only ever wanted to be a good person, Oskar. I only ever wanted a simple life."

Stand with a strong stance.

"Hana, please, just put the gun down."

My arms were starting to ache with the weight of the loaded gun, so I braced myself, taking a deep breath.

"You don't get it, Oskar, do you? I have lost everything. Everything, because of you. And now I have nothing. And I can't live with that anymore."

I was pumped with alcohol and painkillers, but my next move was completely and utterly conducted by the purest form of my own mind. I was brought up Christian, so I asked God to forgive me for every sin I had committed and every sin I will commit today.

Therein, I found it in myself to twist my arm and press the cold steel against the temple of my forehead, closing my eyes tightly and whispering a final prayer.

I missed my family, so, so much.

"Hana, no, please!"

And, finally, pull the trigger.

His bullet seared through my skin, my skull, my memories, my emotions, my control, until it left me hanging in a pit of pure darkness, dead.

And in that moment, in that small, brief and volatile moment, all my fears evaporated as I became part of the dark.

• The end •

Epilogue: Oskar

T hree months.

Three months had passed since she had taken her life, since she had killed herself.

No, she didn't kill herself. It was you. You killed her. Hurriedly, I took a violent swing of vodka.

It was all your fault.

She was gorgeous. I had only seen her smile on a few occasions, but when she did, she glowed. Her smile radiated sunshine for miles on end as though there was nothing in her way. Her angelic doll-like face must have been carved by the hands of Aphrodite herself, because not a single spot of imperfection thrived to taint her beauty.

All. Your. Fault.

She was innocent. She was full of goodness and magnanimity. Her every bone and drop of blood heralded love and compassion and there wasn't a single cell in her body that knew the meaning of maleficence.

But now she's gone.

And though I knew there was no one left in the entire world to remember the goodness she did (for they had all suffered under my affiliated tyranny), I could feel a gap in the universe. I could feel the hole in the world her presence left that her absence haunted. I could feel the hollow of a lifetime without her and it burnt in my chest, more painful than anything I had ever felt before.

And for the first time, alcohol wasn't helping. Nothing I could do could drown away her face from my memory. I was branded by her impression of love and humanity and then with the sour aftertaste of her suffering and pain and hatred.

Hatred for me, of me.

She had every reason to hate me and she rightfully did. She knew I was a vile, disgusting monster even when I thought I was capable of changing for her. I tried my hardest but nothing I could do would have ever been enough to deserve her. And now she's gone. Just like that. Gone.

"We have arrived, Herr Diederich." The car came to an abrupt stop, presenting itself in front of an opulent abode sitting quite happily in the fresh spring air. The driver came round and opened the door to my right, taking his hat in his hands and standing with excellent posture. I exited the car slowly, almost losing balance with the waves of alcohol-induced aches in my head.

It's not just the alcohol, is it?

The last time I was away from the camps, she was with me. She looked just as fantastic as ever and... oh yes, and I told her I loved her. Now, I'm too scared to even say her name.

The double doors of the grand house opened, revealing three neatly dressed maids. They were all visibly older than her and not nearly as thin as she was.

"Heil Hitler," they each greeted me respectfully, accompanied by a small curtsy. I internally grimaced. I took another harsh swing of the drink, hoping it would bleach out those two words from my brain.

All of a sudden, high pitched girlish giggles filled the air (definitely not helping the blaring ache in my head).

"Oskar!" Shouted little Elsa running out of the house, catapulting herself at me. She leaped into my arm and I held her tight at my chest, her giddy smile and hazel eyes filling my vision. Her smile was infectious and somehow stole away the frown that was plastered on my face all day. It was always a delight to see my sister, no matter what the surrounding situation was.

More girlish voices arose as Ada and Carolina came running out of the doors. Carolina ran up to me and hugged my torso tightly, pressing her cheek against my abdomen. I stumbled back a little and tightened my grip on Elsa, who was showering kisses all over my face. I'm sure Carolina has grown two inches since I last saw her. Ada, however, took a more hostile approach and crossed her arms grumpily at my arrival.

"I thought you weren't coming back until Christmas." She said with a sulk.

"I know you missed me." I playfully asserted. They had no real reason to miss me though. I was an awful brother. I was rarely there for their birthdays and only saw them a few times a year. The least they deserved was a decent human as their protector sibling and I couldn't even provide them with that.

Especially Elsa. She was the youngest, just recently turned seven. She was impressionable and vulnerable like any other child her age but she was the strongest little girl I knew. My father gave her so much grief, but she would never end her day without a beautiful smile. I could never choose a favourite sister, but if there was one thing I knew for sure it would be that she was the sister I felt most protective over.

"Did you get us any presents?" Elsa asked, with an optimistic giggle.

"I'm sorry, I would have if I knew I was coming earlier." The disappointment on their faces did not go unnoticed, even on Ada. I put Elsa down, alcohol taking its toll.

"It's okay, we are just happy you're here." Carolina insisted, hugging me tighter.

"I'm not." Ada hadn't changed a bit since I last saw her.

"Did you really think I came without presents?" Elsa gasped with joy and Carolina clapped her hands cheerfully. Even Ada almost looked gleeful. "In the back, go." They ran to the back seat of the car with lightning speed, ready to claim the abundance of chocolates and sweets I managed to pick up on my way here. I was even able to get Ada an early birthday present, hoping I could still get into her good graces.

Leaving the girls to it, I found my way to the front door, though I wobbled and almost fell on the way. At the door, I was finally greeted by the warm smile I had been anticipating for hours on end.

"Son, what are you doing here? Why didn't you tell me you were coming earlier? I would have prepared something, you imbecile!" Mother approached me buoyantly, pulling me into a tight embrace. The smell of cinnamon and freshly laundered clothes enveloped me as I bathed in her solace, hoping this moment would never end.

Would she still hold me like this after she finds out what I have done? Seeing her here, holding her, I felt like a lost little boy again, clinging to his mother in a final act of desperation. I had disappointed her, even though she didn't know it yet. She raised me a good person but somewhere I messed up and I became the monster that would hurt an innocent girl out of selfishness. I didn't deserve such a loving mother.

I didn't deserve anything, but that did not stop me from preying on her and that didn't stop me from almost beating her to death when I did.

Then, when the customary time came to let go of the embrace, I simply couldn't. I clung onto her and held her tight because it was the safest I felt in so long.

"Is this for me?" A little voice sang, finally cutting off our hug. Elsa held a glistening tiara in her hand, swaying back and forth with an impish smile.

"It is." I informed her, genuinely feeling delight as I watched her jump up and down with joy at her new possession.

"Mother, look! It's so pretty! So sparkly!"

"Elsa, go and play with your sisters, please." She ran off obediently and the smile that had unknowingly formed on my face quickly died away.

"Oskar, what's wrong?" Her hand cradled my cheek, and in that moment, in that brief, transient moment, I felt like I was ready for my knees to shatter me to the floor and leave me crying once again.

"Have you been drinking? Darling, it's not even lunchtime yet. What's going on? When was the last time you got some sleep? What the hell happened?" When she saw the lost look in my eye and probably the pain I had been bearing for the past months, she simply retracted her hand and said, "Come inside, we will talk about this later."

Midnight arrived to find the girls fast asleep but I found myself sitting alone on the sofa, hoping the fireplace would offer some warmth.

Her face was already slipping away from my memory even when her shadow was still imprinted there. Chestnut hair with the strikingly blue eyes, the softest lips... but even then, the memory of her felt so distant. I had nothing to remember her by but the constant regret and guilt and anger I felt. No picture, no memento, not even a damn keepsake of our fallacious tryst. Nothing. She was gone, wiped off the face of the planet in a single bullet with nothing left to commemorate her existence.

"Are you ready to talk?" Mother's gentle voice broke me from my train of thoughts as she presented herself in the doorway, a glass of red wine in either hand.

I told her everything. I told her that I used her. I told her that I hurt her. I told her that I let her sister be killed right in front my eyes because I was selfish and I did not want to lose her more.

"But I love her, mother. I promise, I loved her." I tried to convince her. I rested my head on her lap, holding onto her legs tightly as tears came out in floods, wishing it would all just stop.

After hearing all the cruel things I had done, she would believe I wasn't capable of love. I would not be surprised. Maybe I just wasn't. She didn't think I was, so what was to make me believe I was actually capable of loving?

"You hate me too, don't you?"

"Hate you? I could never hate you. I'm disappointed in you, yes, but I could never hate you. I'm not proud of what you did, Oskar, but I'm still your mother and you're still my little boy.

"I'm not going to try and make you feel better for what you did to her, because that's not how I would want someone to be made to feel if they did what you did to any of your sisters, but I will tell you this. You are not an evil person. There is so much good in you and if anything I am at fault for leaving you with your father long enough for him to be able to twist that good into something bad. I know nothing you can do will be able to bring her or her sister back, but you can't drink away your problems and you definitely can't run away from them either."

Hearing her name stung. Part of me was afraid to believe that she no longer existed. Part of me was crumbling at every thought of her existence with immense pain.

Only, whatever I was feeling could not compare to the immense pain I caused her.

For the first time in my nineteen years of life, I didn't believe my mother. I simply could not believe a single shred of good lived in me. I hurt a girl who I told myself I loved more than imaginably possible.

Like I had been told before, I was a monster.

But the worst thing was that now I could not even go back to make it up to her. To make her believe I was capable of being good just for her. She did not believe I was capable of change, anyways. All I could do was lie here, clinging onto my mother as I poured my eyes out on her lap, thinking of all the words that were missing from my mouth when I had the chance to say them to her.

Now, I didn't even have the chance to say 'I'm sorry, Hana Amsel. I'm sorry I fell in love with you and I'm sorry I let your castle fall to ruins.'